Unapologetically Nessa

Dedication

Thank you to my readers:
None of this is truly possible without you. Thank you for following me on this journey and to many more with you beside me.

Table of Contents

Shots!
Awkward
Greyson
Disaster Date
Lightweight
It was ONE Drink
Calliope
What to Wear?
Date Night
Bridget
Nightcap
Day Date
Sample World
Confrontation
Night at the Bar
Sad Song
Delusional
Briar
Sweet Revenge
The Aftermath
Nothing to Talk About
Party Time
Caught
I Warned YOU
Tears
Hello, Kayden
Who Is He?
This Time it's Different
Guess What…
Tease
You're a What?!
A Last Wild Night
The Future Mrs. Grey
Get Ready

Wow...
Mine
Forever Etched
Into the Future

Warning: Contains strong language/adult situations

This is a work of fiction.
Names, characters, places, and incidents either are the product of the author's imagination or are used fictitiously. Any resemblance to actual persons, living or dead, events, or locales are entirely coincidental.

Copyright © 2020
All rights reserved.

No part of this book may be reproduced in any form on by an electronic or mechanical means, including information storage and retrieval systems, without permission in writing from the publisher, except by a reviewer who may quote brief passages in a review.

Shots!

"Wooooo! Spring Break, bitches! Hey sexy, get me six shots of tequila for me and my best friend here!"

I decided to up the ante by leaning over in my skintight little black dress, with its sheer paneling in all the right places, showcasing my amazing set of tits.

I bring it home by gently biting my crimson-stained lip, "Please…" I say watching him adjust himself as he sets the glasses in front of me. I smile as he pours the amber liquid into the crystal glasses. As he finishes, I reach into my bra to pull out the cash, but he holds his hand up.

"No charge, beautiful."

Nice, well I have to give him something.

I grab him by his neck and pull his lips to mine. He tastes like mint with a hint of tobacco, a smoker…eh, I can deal with that. He can puff away after the amazing sex session I'm sure we'd have.

I pull back and smile, "Thanks, lover boy." I jot down my number on a napkin, press it against his rock-solid abs and drag it down into his pants…and not his pockets. He gasps at my bold move.

"Don't lose it, you only get one chance." I wink before he attends to the next customer. Maybe I'll have some fun tonight after all.

I look over to my best friend Kam, she is definitely drunk, for her, painfully so. She's such a lightweight, Goddess help her, but she tries to hang on for me.

"Nessa, I don't know if I can down three more, I can feel my liver dying!"

I pass her a single shot and cradle the remainder, "Don't worry, buddy, I'll take the rest."

I slam down the first two before I feel the hands of someone wrap around my waist. I can't see him, so I use Kam as my eyes. She looks him over and nods her head in approval, which means he's hot, so I turn around to see a tall drink of water with dark hair and smoldering eyes. His rough hands squeeze my sides as he asks me to dance. I agree but slide over my remaining shots to Kam. "Watch my babies until I get back." She laughs as I follow the handsome guy to the dance floor of the only bar in town, Jack's.

It's a country saloon themed bar which correlates to this small, quiet town that is Lovenshire.

One horse town? There probably isn't a horse within a twenty-mile radius, all the ranches are north of town nestled near the mountains for easy access to the grazing trails. Besides, this place is surrounded by deep, luscious forests, the kind that can hold even the most mythical of creatures and more.

I seem to enjoy the music more than my partner, not because he isn't a fine partner, it's just I get caught up in the tempo as if I'm alone. I sway my hips, dancing around, keeping a watchful eye on my best friend. I can't lie, I always feel a pang of sadness when I watch her pine for true love. Kam is a beautifully old-fashioned soul and that is what makes her a rare catch.

Me, on the other hand, I'm way more interested in having fun, taking said fun home, and tying it to my bed rather than finding true love.

I'm thrown back to the present when his hands work away from caressing my hips and glide down to my ass and he squeezes firmly making me jump a little.

"Whoa there, cowboy. I don't even know your name! Give me that before you go sampling the goods."

He smiles, and what a gorgeous smile it is, pulling my hand up for a chaste kiss. "The name's Dallas and what's yours, gorgeous."

Well, that killed it.

I laughed out loud before I turned around and headed back to my seat. Kam is shocked to see me leave him standing alone on the dance floor and I can only assume that his face is equally surprised.

"What the hell, Nessa?! Why did you leave him on the dance floor?"

I slam down two more shots, wanting to savor the last one. I spin around, "His name is Dallas, you know how I feel about guys named after towns. Hard pass…"

I take the last shot back and observe the crowd. Mr. City man disappeared to another part of the club, probably trying his luck elsewhere.

Kam just shakes her head and takes the shot she's been babysitting for at least three hours now. She took it without a chaser so I'm pretty proud of her.

"I know, but he was drop-dead gorgeous, Nes. Who cares if he was named after a town? Even I was having naughty thoughts about what I would do to him." She licks her lips and smiles.

I do a hard eye roll, "Yeah no, remember Austin? Or Jackson…Denver, oh he was a change of pace because I caught him with…hmm, oh, Jefferson! So, no thank you to city named assholes!"

I change the subject by quickly dragging her to the dance floor for some best friend fun.

Soon we are the center of every man's attention as we playfully grind on each other. Kam is dressed in an equally tight red dress that sits slightly longer than mine but she's also tall and statuesque. She looks like a model who could easily have any man she wants.

Knowing we have the attention I decide to turn up the flames by sliding my hands down to Kam's hips, grinding myself against her. The sound of a glass dropping echoes from behind us, I can only imagine one of these guys is so overwhelmed by our sexy moves that he's lost all his motor skills.

Kam turns around and rocks against me to whisper, "Hey, you got a fan. Three o'clock with the red button down and wranglers."

UGH, really?! Wranglers? I feel the automatic eye-roll come on because Wranglers totally scream country boy, and here EVERYBODY is a country boy, it gets old. I want a motorcycle-riding bad boy or even a sports car enthusiast, something that has nothing to do with my country ass surroundings.

Still curious, I decided to scratch my itch and I turned to see the sexiest country fed farm boy I have ever seen. He's got to be six foot six with wicked sapphire blue eyes and as our eyes meet, I watch his lips form into a radiant smile, accompanied by a hot set of dimples.

"Fuck me." The words slip out.

"What?!" Kam freezes, staring at me.

"Not you, Mr. Dimples at the bar. He is absolutely gorgeous. Oh yes, I am going to enjoy this. Back me up, bestie."

I saunter from the stage up to the bar standing next to him as he pretends to watch the dance floor. I can feel the heat of his gaze on my ass. I step up on the metal bar so I can further bend over to catch the bartender's attention along with my admirer.

The bartender finally notices all my curves on display, luckily, it's a different one than earlier. He throws his towel across his shoulder and leans towards me looking me over.

"What can I get you, love?"

Just then Mr. Gorgeous turns and boldly wraps his arm around my waist, pulling me onto his lap and his...oh my! I don't fight it as both arms wrap around me.

"The lady will have a Long Island Iced Tea and I'll have a bourbon, straight up." The bartender nods but I stop him, "Oh, and water for my best friend." I hear Kam sigh in relief, I don't think she can even inhale the scent of alcohol right now.

I slide off his lap to face my Casanova, "Pretty confident, huh? What's your name, handsome?"

Please not a city. Please not a city.

He takes my hand and kisses it gently, "The name is Greyson beautiful, and you?"

"Nessa and this is my best friend, Kam." Kam nods in acknowledgment before grabbing her water and heading to the patio outside for some fresh air.

He places his fingertips on my chin to face him, "So Nessa, what's a guy have to do to get a girl's number?" I look him up and down, licking my lips before I smile devilishly.

Later, I slam against my door, laughing uncontrollably probably a lot louder than I should be at two in the morning. I'm struggling to get my key into the lock. Finally, after a deep sigh and some concentration, the door swings open. The AC cools and soothes my overheated face after a night of dancing. I throw my keys into the bowl and start peeling off my ridiculously tight dress. Finally free, I sigh loudly, "Oh thank Goddess that feels so liberating! I'll be right back then you can use the bathroom."

I wash the night from my face, brush my teeth, and wash my hands. It feels so good to be fresh-faced. I can't help but yawn as I open the door.

"Okay, free to use." I plop face down on my bed until I hear the door open again and the bed dips. I take a moment to plug in my phone before I roll over facing Kam.

"I had such a fun time; we have to do it again sometime soon."

"Don't push it, missy, I still need to open my studio today and function as an adult. I am not the party girl I once was."

Kam lays down facing me and smiles but then frowns. "Do you realize that four guys hit on you and I got nothing. Look at me! I wore the dress you picked out, why can't I find anyone?" She groans into the pillow and I rub her back until she faces me again.

I see her eyes start to well with tears, but I won't let her feel down, "It's true love darling. You're not one for casual hookups or one-night stands and word travels fast in our sleepy little town so all these guys who live here know unless they are willing to settle down to not even glance your way. You're a gem, Kammi Kam."

She rolls her eyes as she turns away to go to sleep.

Awkward

The next morning, I whine as I open one eye to check the time: 8:30 am. I know by seeing the empty bed, that Kam is already back at her place getting ready to go to work. I envy her, at the age of 22, Kamari Lee is a thriving business owner of her own art studio and she has quite the talent!

Of course, as her best friend I'm proud to own her first two pieces and they are stunning.

Though the town is no big metropolitan she was able to pick up steady business especially from Mr. and Mrs. Preston, a lovely couple who have grown to love her artwork. I love them as well; they are just the cutest elderly couple you could ever meet. Their mate bond shows anytime they're together.

Oh, did I forget to mention that I am a werewolf, well, part werewolf and part silver witch?

Yes, I am quite badass.

I, Vanessa Ann Vanderbilt, have spent my entire life under the great Cheshire Pack. Our pack is known for the top trained and most powerful warriors under the great Alpha Mitchell Miller. I only lived on pack ground the first five years before my family decided to move down to Lovenshire, but I always come back for the events, training, and mandatory meetings.

The only drawback is that I can't tell my best friend what I am, it's forbidden. I'm sure because someone from the past messed it up for everyone. Anyway, the rules state that the human must be their mate or figure it out on their own. So, when I have to go to the packhouse I always say I have a date with some random person I met at work. Lucky for me I work at the café, so it's possible to meet people just stopping through.

I flip over on my bed and hit a piece of paper with my hand.

Check your phone, Miss Popularity. See you after work. Buzz me later, Kam.

I force myself to turn over again to grab my phone which lights up with unread messages:

Unknown: Hey, sweet cheeks this is Colby, bartender from last night. Hit me up when you're ready for me to take you to dinner and whatever else... Talk to you later, gorgeous.

Unknown #2: Good morning, sunshine. This is Greyson and I could not get your beautiful face out of my head. Allow me to wine and dine you tonight and I promise you won't regret it. Call me, baby.

I sit up slightly to think of a response and who the lucky recipient will be of the win-a-date-with-Nessa. For a second, I think about Kam and her traditional ways. My girl is a no-nonsense kind of girl and on the hunt for true love. I should be too since I am gifted with a mate by the Moon Goddess herself, I just have to find him but where's the fun in that?!

I finally decide on the winner and send him a reply:

Well, good morning gorgeous man I'm glad I was on your mind torturing you all night. I would love for you to wine and dine me, say tonight, 8 pm? Until then, stud.

I laugh as my phone buzzes almost immediately. I look down:

G: Absolutely I can't wait to see the woman that was in my fantasies all night. Send me your address and I'll pick you up.

I can't help but laugh, typing in my address, except with Kam's apartment number instead of mine. We live right next door to each other, but it was a safety tactic we adopted in case of a crazy stalker situation, the other could say that she simply moved away.

I hop in the shower to begin yet another day at the café. What can I say, it's a living.

"Nessa! Table eight needs syrup, table three needs sugar, and nobody has even looked at table seven, now go!" I sigh as I gather everything to satisfy the tables. The cook, Griff, grunts out the orders to me.

I maneuver the tables with ease, "Here's your syrup all warmed up for you like you always like it, Merv. Sugar for Timothy's tea, only three packets! Welcome to Tidal Cafe, what can I get you to drink?" I look up to a pair of familiar eyes.

"Good morning, sweet cheeks."

Colby. Shit…shit shit shit!

"So formal are we but you weren't when you were sliding your number into my pants last night, the one time I don't wear underwear. And I'll be honest, you created a problem that I had to take care of, sweetheart. Did you get my text this morning?" Colby puts his arm up against the booth waiting for my reply.

"One, I am at work so I'd like to keep my job and two, that was last night and yes I did get your message this morning, I woke up late and couldn't respond, sorry."

He sits forward and smiles, "It's okay, I was lucky enough to run into you this morning to see if you wanted to go out tonight? Maybe a movie or something?" He eyes me over in my uniform and bites his lip, anxiously awaiting my response.

UGH, I hate doing this, but it has to be done.

"I'm sorry Colby but I already have a date tonight, somebody beat you to it. Let's talk later, I am super busy right now as you can see. I'll send Melissa to bring you your drink."

Without another word I turn and head to the back of the kitchen. I signal my co-worker Melissa over. "Hey Mel, can you cover table seven, please." I usually try not to ask Melissa for anything but I'm desperate.

Melissa pops her gum and looks over at the table through the kitchen window. "Holy smokes, he is gorgeous, why aren't you serving that handsome devil?"

"Because he was my bartender last night and I gave him my number, it's a long story, but somebody else already asked me out. It's awkward, just please, do me this favor!" She nods and heads to his table as I inhale and exhale loudly. It's already going to be a drama-filled day, I can't wait to tell Kam about this.

Greyson

Kam laughs uncontrollably on her couch as I zip up my form-fitting dress and slip on my sexy cardigan. "It isn't *that* funny, Kam!"

"Oh, but it is! Both guys text you and you pick one only to run into the other one at your job! HAHAHAHAHAHA!!!!"

"You are a terrible friend, you know that?" I go into the bathroom to finish my makeup. I keep my makeup simple. The dress is the wow factor tonight, there is no need for me to go for the kill on the first date.

Kam leans against the door and sighs. "Oh, Nessa you know I couldn't help but tease. You handled the situation just fine and if he never texts again then so be it, he wasn't for you. Now let's focus on the task at hand, 'Operation Get Some from Greyson' That man...wow." She exhales forcefully while fanning herself.

"I can see the heart eyes on your face, back off missy, he's mine." We share a laugh, "I know that besides, he's not my type, just nice to look at."

I put down my makeup brush, "And how will you know when you find your one?"

She taps her chest where her heart is and smiles, "It'll tell me all I need." She walks into the kitchen to pop some popcorn for her solo movie night.

Hearing a knock at the door and having just sat down, Kam groans as she walks over to answer it.

She is met by a handsomely dressed Greyson with his perfect smile. "Hello, Greyson, nice to see you again, please come in." He walks in and sits on the sofa, unbuttoning his suit jacket.

"Nice to see you again, Kam. I didn't know you two were roommates?"

Kam comes back and places the popcorn bowl in her lap, wrapping her favorite blanket around herself. "Oh, we're not, this is my place we don't give out our apartments on the first date. It's a thing we do."

His eyebrow raises before I make my entrance causing his jaw to hit the floor. Nailed it.

"Well, hello, angel face, you look stunning." He kisses my hand and twirls me about to get the full view. The dress is fitted and accentuates my killer curves.

I blush as his arms wrap around me in a hug.
"Hello, handsome. You ready?" His hand grazes my ass and I yelp, I start to blush wildly.

Disaster Date

Later that night:

"You did WHAT?!" Kam shouts from the top of her lungs at me as I peel myself out of my dress.

"I slept with him, so what? Why is this shocking news, you saw him? He wined and dined me, so I wanted to see if he had potential..."

"AND?! Well, don't leave me hanging!"

I wash my face and while patting it dry, I turn to her. "And, I should have gone out with Colby, at least I felt what he was offering, and it was nice, definitely doable. But Greyson was all about himself and you know that is a major turnoff for me, might as well be named after a city he was that bad...oh, and quick, too. I gave him a second chance...and a third but still nothing. Had to finish the job myself in his bathroom because I didn't want to hurt his feelings. Such a tragedy, too."

Kam shakes her head in disappointment, "Damn, that sucks. Well, you still have a chance with Colby."

I grin widely while pulling my hair up into a ponytail, "That I do because he texted me between rounds two and three with boring-ass Greyson so I said I would go out with him sometime next week."

Kam looks shocked, "You texted in-between rounds of sex?"

I scoff as we settle into the living room for an after-date movie, "That hardly counted as sex so yes, I did." We can't help but bust out laughing. "Nessa, you're a mess and I love you for it."

The following Friday, I went out with Colby and I came back to report the details to Kam. She takes in the smile plastered across my face as I lean against the door.

"Hmmm, I take it this went better than what's his name?"

I nod proudly while putting my jacket in the closet, "Mhmm, so much better even after the fourth and fifth round. He's got the stamina of a champion stallion! Wow...I just might be in love." I stagger to the sofa, my legs achingly weak from pleasure.

Kam can't contain her amusement, "Oh you're in love alright but not with him, just a part of him."

She tosses the blanket from behind her as I wrap myself with it.

"And I will love it over and over and over again, you hear me?! Are my pajamas still in your dresser drawer? I'm too tired to go to my place besides, we can have some girl time."

"Nessa, your place is 15 steps away."

"Well, when you've been worked over like I have your legs get a little weak..."

"Okay...TMI..."

I wobble to her dresser grabbing some pajama bottoms and a tank top joining her back in the living room.

Kam looks over at me and I can tell she has something on her mind.

"Umm Nessa? Something happened earlier today that I want to talk to you about, John Michael asked me out today. Yeah, he came into the studio and said he had no purpose other than to ask the beautiful owner out on a date."

She's fidgeting with her hands, too nervous to even bring up the situation but she needs my advice.

I leaned forward almost falling out of my damn chair in anticipation. "And? Talk about keeping people in suspense! What else did he say?!" She shrugs her shoulders, "Nothing much after that he was waiting for my answer. I told him I'd think about it. But isn't he messing with Bridget?"

"Girl, who isn't messing with the town slut? But I think that if he put that much effort into coming down to your shop to ask you out, I don't see why not! Did you give him your number?"

She nods while checking her phone, "Yeah, he's been texting me since then."

I snatch her phone and scroll through their conversation just reading his responses. I know hers are shy and stoic.

(7:38) J: Hello beautiful

(8:18) J: Hope you have thought about my proposal, I would love to take you out

(8:20) J: Don't keep me waiting long, princess.

(9:05) J: I'm calling at 10pm for my answer, I hope you have one.

I checked my watch, it was 9:55pm.

"He's going to call in five minutes! What are you going to say?!"

Again, she shrugs her shoulders. "I think he's cute but if he's messing with Bridget then I can't, for some reason, she doesn't like me and honestly, I don't like her, either. I don't want any confrontation because she thinks I took her man."

I scoff loudly, "Screw that promiscuous bitch, this is about you and him, no one else. Tell me, what do you WANT to do?"

She's quiet for a moment before a mischievous smile forms across her face, "I want to go out with him."

Just then her phone buzzes. I signal for her to put it on speakerphone so I can hear.

"Hello?"

"Hello, gorgeous. So, will you let me take you out tomorrow night? I promise it will be the perfect date."

"It doesn't have to be perfect; you just have to be you. I'd love to go out with you, John."

"Thank you, beautiful, I can't wait to see your gorgeous smile. Be ready at 7pm, okay?"

"Okay."

"See you tomorrow sunshine. Sweet dreams."

"Goodnight."

I can't help but squeal like a pig, "Oh my goodness! Does my Kammi Kam have a date tomorrow?!" She joins me in shrieking, and we start a pillow fight, chucking pillows at each other until we collapse, laughing giddily.

"Oh my gosh, this is the first date in so long, I hope this works out Nessa. I…I really like him."

I pull her to her feet as we dance around celebrating her upcoming date.

"Well, it all starts with the first date and I will be here to make you look spectacular! You gave him my apartment number, right?" She nods.

"Well let's get to bed, you have work in the morning."

"WE have work in the morning." She casually reminds me.

I sigh, "Oh, yeah right. I haven't mysteriously won the lottery today, bummer."

Lightweight

I head to the packhouse before my shift later this morning. I told Kam I was going to visit the falls for some much-needed thinking time.

I pull into the packhouse and make my way inside. Not really paying attention, I find myself barreling into someone then falling on my ass.

"HEY, watch it!"

The figure stops and turns around. "Sorry, Nes..." He sniffs around me. "You always smell so amazing but it's not you, per se, I know your scent, it's someone you hang around. It's an arousing aroma..." He inhales deeply and his eyes flicker before returning to normal.

"Look, Miller, the only person I hang with is my best friend who is human, it can only be her but you're too late she has a date tonight and hopefully he's the one she falls madly in love with."

He backs down and walks away. Kayden Miller is set to inherit the Alpha title from his dad, but everyone knows that his current goal is to find his

Luna before being crowned, he's borderline obsessed with finding her, kind of like Kam.

Anyway, I finish my yearly assessment with the pack trainers, take a shower and head to work. When I walk into the café I'm immediately confronted by Tabitha, another waitress I work with.

"Girl! Who is Colby? He left you these beautiful orchids." She points to a purple vase with a silver bow.

"Wow...they're beautiful." Tabitha hands me the card that was neatly placed against the vase. I open the envelope to retrieve it.

Thank you for the wonderful evening, let's do it again. :) I'll call you, beautiful. Colby

I find myself swooning as I recall the events of that hot and torrid night. I open my phone to text him.

N: Thank you for the flowers, you really know how to spoil a girl.

C: Obviously, but you make it so easy. How about the movies on Friday?

N: Absolutely and this time you can pick me up at MY place.

C: I feel honored, talk to you later doll face.

*N: *kisses**

I turn back to Tabitha and before she can even squeak out a word, I hold up my hand to stop her before she continues her barrage of questions. I take one more moment to inhale the scent of the flowers before tying my apron and heading out to my tables, it's going to be a long shift.

Later that evening, as I attempt to finish Kam's makeup, I stop and shake my head at her. "Stop fidgeting Kamari! I'll never get you done in time!"

Kam flinches, not only because I'm calling her by her entire name, but also every time I get close with the tweezers to apply the faux eyelashes, she becomes unnerved.

I sigh in frustration. "Okay, just close your eyes and I'll tell you when to open them."

Kam also sighs but it is full of nerves, "I'm so tense Nessa, what if he thinks I'm dull or not up to his speed? I don't think I can do this!" She starts to hyperventilate.

I grab her by her arms, "Hey, stop it. Let me tell you something I always want you to remember. You are an amazing girl, beautiful, strong and with the biggest heart, I've ever seen. The man who sweeps you off your feet will be damned lucky in finding you! John happens to have the luck tonight so go have fun, enjoy the company of that gorgeous man and maybe even..."

Kam gives me 'the look' and cuts me off. "Not a chance Nessa, not on the first date." She calms enough to let me finish up her makeup.

I stand back and beam, "There. Simplistic because you my friend are a stunningly classic beauty. Now put on that wrap dress and use my strappy tan wedges in the corner, he'll be here any minute!" She squeals and runs into the bathroom to change.

Hearing a knock at my door, I go to answer it, "Hello, John Michael, come in." He looks confused as I step out of his way so he can walk in.

"Hey Vanessa, I didn't know you two were roommates?" I sit in the recliner closest to the tv. "Oh, we don't tell people where we live on our first dates, this is my place. She should be just about ready."

Not a moment later, the bathroom door clicks softly open and Kam comes out in a royal purple wrap dress and my tan peep-toe wedges. She looks down shyly as he approaches her. Her breathing hitches when his shoes come into her view on the floor.

"Wow, Kamari, you look amazing. I'm one lucky man." He holds her chin up to meet her gaze. "Always keep your head up, beautiful." She beams as they share a sweet moment. "You ready? Let's go." She grabs her clutch and smiles at me.

"You know the usual, text me when you get back or knock on my door...unless you're busy. Have fun kiddos!" She glares at me and I know she's blushing even though she hides it well.

My phone starts buzzing, and I stretch over the chair to reach the table I put it on, "Hello?"

"Hey, it's Greyson…"

Dalila, my inner wolf, starts laughing loud. Dalila is always painfully honest, she's one wolf with absolutely no filter, just like me but worse because she has no reason for remorse.

D: Hell no. Tell that three-minute loser to bug off, you got a real man now.

"Yes, Greyson?" I feign interest in this interaction.

"I just wanted to get a second chance, I know the night didn't turn out...well, but I had been dealing with some issues and..."

"Greyson, Greyson, I'm sorry you were having erectile issues or whatever, I'm also sorry I gave you three chances to redeem yourself but I am not sorry that I managed to finish myself off and give myself an amazing orgasm, I mean someone had to. It was an interesting time, but it won't happen again, there are too many men who can respond like I want and need. Best wishes to you, Greyson. Have a nice life." I hang up not giving him a chance to respond.

By then Dalila is rolling on the floor laughing in my subconscious.

D: You forgot to tell him they got meds for that, yo! And another one bites the dust...next up, Colby and his at-bat is spot on every single time. Maybe we can call for a sample before Friday night?

"Shut up, D, we don't want to look desperate!"

D: But...he was sooo good.

Dalila licks her lips recalling their date.

I try to ignore her ramblings as I settle in for the night, I could use a good action film to wash away the memory.

A while later, I don't know how long because I fell asleep, I hear someone knocking at my damn door. At this hour it could only be Kam. I open the door and my best friend is giggling as she falls forward wrapping me up in a tight hug.

"Oh Nes, I had the best time!" I can smell the alcohol on her breath as I notice a chuckling John Michael behind her holding her up slightly.

"Jesus John, you got her drunk?" I narrow my eyes at him.

"Seriously? It was a tequila sunrise, ONE tequila sunrise."

Kam leans forward and whispers, but it's just loud yelling in a whisper tone.

"I'm totally going to bang him, he's soooo hot! Mmm…" She looks back at her tall and handsome date then winks at him.

"O--kay! John, ignore her and you, missy, it's time for sleep, go lay in my bed."

Kam takes a step forward before turning around and falling forward but he catches her. She places her hands on his broad chest as his arms wrap around her waist.

"Ooh, my hero! Okay handsome, next time you, me, my place and a lot of sex!" She pulls him down for an intense kiss. At first, he seemed shocked but then his hands started roaming her body, gripping her in all the right places. They break away and she puts her finger against his lip.

"Okay, I have to go to bed now but text me you got home, okay, sexy?" He nods as she makes her way to my room. I listen and hear her plop on the bed as I turn back to him, chuckling.

"That must have been one strong drink."

"Yeah, if I had known I would have told them to lighten up. Did she mean what she said?"

"She may be tipsy, but Kamari is no liar. She really likes you John so think long and hard before you pursue with intent because she's too rare of a gem for you to be screwing her over. You know her reputation as sweet and innocent so let's keep it that way, huh?"

"You mean she's a virgin?"

I roll my eyes hard. "Men, all you think about is sex. No, you moron, I meant her soul is pure, her intentions and her love. She's not a wandering slut like Bridget, all she wants is happiness, now...can you give that because if not then end this now!"

He reflects on the night drawing a smile, "She is special, and I want to be the one to show her." I just nod as he turns around to head home. I close the door and shut everything down to join Kam in bed.

"He had better be or there will be hell to pay."

It was ONE drink

After a groggy wake-up, I hear moaning and not the good kind, "Help meeeee...the pain! Ugh, what did I drink last night?" Kam sits up and immediately shields herself from the traitorous sun.

I laugh hysterically, "One drink apparently! I have got to get your tolerance up but a bit of warning, you told John you were going to 'bang' him because he was so hot."

Kam looks mortified, as she slams the pillow over her face, screaming out in humiliation.

"I can never look him in the face again! I remember being really touchy-feely at the restaurant and then we went to Jack's for a mo--tequila sunrise, I had tequila, you know what that does to me! UGHHH!"

"Apparently, now he knows too, this is retribution for you laughing at me about the Colby/Greyson situation."

I think my uncontrollable laughter is a little too much for her liking as she tries to smother me with her pillow.

"This is serious, what am I going to do now? I can't avoid him in this small ass town, he probably thinks I'm so weird! This is why I don't date...I just want someone to sweep me off my feet and carry me away to my 'happy ever after' without the awkward dating part."

"That's not how that works, anyway that's how you weed out the assholes, jerks, and the quickdraws...he wasn't bothered by your behavior, in fact, it may have worked in your favor. I wasn't trying to look but he was sporting a hard-on when he left. Anyway, I talked to him about you and how innocent you are."

"Nessa, you know I'm not a virgin..."

"NO! That's not what I meant, jeez he thought that too, maybe you are right for each other. I meant your heart is pure and he should think really long and hard because if he hurts you, I am going to hurt him...bad."

"He was a perfect gentleman the entire night, Nes. It was me and apparently the tequila who had all eyes on me on the dance floor." I could see the memories were flooding back just by her expression. "Oh dear lord, I think all his friends saw me, too." She smacks her hand to her head.

"So what?"

"So what?! A guy's friends always give their opinion of the girl they date or take out, they probably told him to never call me again."

I sit up and look at Kam who is shaking her head. "Trust me, he doesn't care what they say, before this day is out you will hear from him because he is very much interested in you. In all of you, the crazy girl, the jokester, the emotional wreck when she watches Titanic. He is more than eager to see you again, don't worry."

Kam sighs and checks her phone; it seems he texted her once he got home but it's no short text.

(12:45am) J: Hey doll face, I'm home. Never had anyone care that I made it safely so thank you, gorgeous. I'm coming by the shop today, just because I can't wait to see you again. Until then, JM.

I take in her face as she blushes wildly, and I grab her phone to see why. "See! I was right. That big heart of yours will get you snatched up in no time."

Kam squeals as she tells me she is heading to her house to get ready for work, undoubtedly changing her clothes from her usual leggings and sweatshirt style, because of a special patron that will be coming by, and we are not talking about The Preston's'.

I can't help but shake my head, "My girl, the hopeless romantic and me the...wait, what day is it?" I check my phone and lick my lips, "Ooh, and me with a date with Colby tonight. Mmm, this is going to be fun." I start getting ready for work, hoping and praying for the time to rush by so I can be on my date already.

Calliope

I get in and just as I set my belongings in my cubby my phone rings.

(9:04 am) C: Come to table 6, gorgeous.

I peer out to see Colby at table six, he's dressed in a dark blue suit and no tie, classic and modern at the same time. I finish tying my apron quickly as he stands to greet me, his smile is mesmerizing.

"Good morning, sunshine. I brought you these to remind you of our date tonight."

He hands me a dozen yellow roses from seemingly out of nowhere. I gasp, catching the attention of some of the customers.

"Colby, they're absolutely beautiful, thank you." I inhale the wonderful scent.

"They aren't as beautiful as you, now, I'm running late for work. I'll see you tonight, be ready at 7 pm?" I agree and he places the softest kiss to my lips, I'm internally melting. "Until later." He turns to leave and is shoulder checked by someone but doesn't care to confront the guy and walks away.

The other guy turns back around and it's none other than...

"Greyson." I huff and turn to walk back to the kitchen.

"Nessa, don't walk away from me! Why did you hang up on me?! Who gave you those? Are you already seeing someone else? Was it that guy who just walked out?"

I can feel the irritation build as he rambles off questions. "Not that it's any of your business, but since you want to cause a scene, yes, another guy gave me his number the same night you did and I messaged him between rounds two and three with you to set up our date and he had no problem pleasing me, several times."

Without thinking, he grabs my arm, spinning me around forcibly. Dalila starts to stir, and she is not happy.

D: That son of a bitch has a millisecond before I castrate that limp dick of his!

A low growl creeps up my throat and I know my eyes change to a stunning dark silver, a voice comes from my lips, I have been trying to keep *her* at bay but she's not having it.

"Nessa is not in control and her wolf isn't either, I think you know who I am. I suggest you unhand me before you take your final breath. She told you it didn't work out and I'm trying to be civil, but I could rip you apart. Let's just part ways and be cordial. Got. It?!"

I close my eyes as I gain control back.

Greyson let's go of me, visibly petrified, it's well known to the pack of my hybrid status but very few have seen *her* and lived. I only let her out in intense situations, if you think Dalila is hostile, you don't want to meet Calliope.

I finally calm her down enough to regain full control. "Just leave Greyson, please, you're going to cause me to lose my job," I whisper and once again try to turn around and walk away. Thank goodness my boss and most of the people who witnessed the incident were part of the pack.

"Vanessa wait...I-I'm sorry, I really am. You're right I was just reacting to my bruised ego. You're a great girl and deserve what you want. Forgive me?"

I eye him carefully and then relent, "No hard feelings, Greyson. I'm sure you'll find the right person, someday." He opens his arms and I step into the hug. Calliope is not happy with my decision to keep him intact, but I ignore her.

"You are one hot firecracker, Nessa. I don't know who'll be able to tame you, but he'll have fun trying."

We share a laugh before he leaves the diner.

What to Wear?

Later that night I mull over both of my options,

"What do you think, Kam...short, tight, and red... or LBD?"

Kam looks at me confused, "It's the movies, Nes it'll be dark so why dress so sexy?"

I can't help but laugh while I shake my head, "Oh, dear, to drive him crazy of course! It'll guarantee a grope fest once those lights go down and that's exactly what I want. I'll tease him with little touches here and there until he's dying to throw me against the wall and..."

"I GOT IT... well, in that case, can't go wrong with the little black dress and that new leather jacket you got three days ago." I toss the red dress to the side, take the winning dress and the jacket into the bathroom.

There's a knock on the door and Kam says she'll get it.

Kam opens it to a dozen roses being nearly shoved in her face. "Whoa!"

"Hello, gor--oh, Kam I'm so sorry!"

I hear her snicker, "Don't worry, I promise I won't be here every time you come to take her out. I was just helping coordinate the outfit."

He smiles as he takes a single rose from the bunch, "Well, then this is for you for being such a great friend. You guys share something special and that is an important relationship to have."

She blushes, "Why, thank you."

She takes the rose just as I step out. "Are you hitting on my bestie, too? Don't you even consider a threesome, she will not participate as much as I want her to."

Kam's mouth drops open, "WHAT?!"

I just shake my head, "I kid, I kid. So, lover boy are the rest of those for me?"

Kam takes her rose and sits down, "Yup, this one is mine and thank you, Colby, it was sweet of you."

He hands over the near dozen red roses and places a kiss to my cheek, holy hell my temperature is already on the rise. "Yes, beautiful these are for you. I was thanking your friend for being there before our dates. Anyway, you look hot, too hot for the movies. Are you planning to seduce me?"

I put the flowers in a vase, grab my jacket and purse and look over my shoulder, undressing him with my eyes, "Planning to? Ha, already have."

I laugh as I wait by the door for him. He glances over at Kam and gulps.

He walks over and opens the door for me, I saunter past him and out the door.

"Have fun, you two!" Kam shouts out just as her phone buzzes.

(7:12 pm) J: I miss you. You're the best part of my day.

I bet she is smiling from ear to ear, blush rising from her cheeks, she can feel the heat.

(7:13 pm) K: Aww I miss you, too. Come watch a movie with me, same address but the apartment to the right.

As always, I know she will lock my door before she heads back to her apartment to get ready for her own date.

(7:17 pm) J: See you in twenty minutes then. I'll bring the non-alcoholic drinks ;P

(7:17 pm) K: Oh, ha ha. Just hurry up, I want to cuddle!

She texts me to let me know, then she takes a quick shower and puts on her pajamas as she awaits John's arrival.

Date Night

Downstairs, I gasp as we walk up to a vintage Camaro, jet black with an underlying blue tint. Oh my Goddess I am in love, "Oh wow, this is one sexy beauty. I love Camaros! They are such a hot car; I've always wanted to..."

He winks as he opens my door, "We'll have plenty of time for that, darling." He climbs in the driver's seat, revving the engine.

Wanting to tease him, I seductively cross my legs, shortening the length of my dress. I lean in close and whisper, "Show me what this bad boy can do." I kiss his neck and he let out a growl before shifting into gear and going from 0 to 70 in four and a half seconds and I'm intoxicated by the speed. I wanted him to pull over at make-out point and take me for a ride, but I have to play it coy.

We arrive at the theater in no time and I'm breathless from the exhilaration, my breath ragged, and my eyes filled with excitement among other things. He looks over and smirks, "Now gorgeous, show me what those lips can do." I immediately eye his lap while biting my lip, but he corrects me, "As fun as that sounds, we wouldn't make the movie, I meant a kiss, sweetheart." He taps his cheek and I laugh then I lean forward planting several sweet kisses before going in for the kill. I slide into his lap and tug at his hair as we battle for control, eventually, he takes over or I let him. His hands tease me in the worst way, if this weren't a public venue…

I pull back, panting hard. "Wow, we should go, or else I'm going to cause a scene."

He goes to open my door and sticks out his hand for me to take. "Thank you." He kisses my hand, "You're so welcome." He wraps his arm around my waist as we walk up to the ticket booth.

"You know we never talked about which movie we were going to see."

I look at all the options "Hmm, well for one, no chick flicks, there's the new action or the new horror movie. Let's do horror, I love a good scare besides, it'll be really sexy to have you hold me and protect me from the fictional scary monster, whatever it is. I may even end up in your lap."

That earns another growl from him. "I didn't peg you for a horror fan."

"Oh honey, you have no idea." He pays for the tickets and we head to the concession stand.

Meanwhile:

"Oh, god John...mmm, it feels so good. Oh, right there! Harder baby, harder!"

Kam is panting as she looks down at a smirking John Michael. "Baby you sound so sexy; I could do this forever just to hear your cute little moans. All you have to do is pay me in kisses." He continues rubbing her feet as she melts into his strong hands. She stretches her neck, rubbing it as she sighs loudly. "I spent four hours straight working on Mrs. Preston's painting today and my feet are so sore, thank you, baby."

He flashes his impeccable smile that makes her swoon, "Anything for you, Princess." As soon as the words leave his lips, I hear a scream from the movie we are barely watching, and I jump scream right into his lap.

There is an awkward silence before he leans forward for a kiss, an innocent peck. He pulls back gauging my response as I answer by leaning in for a deeper kiss. Five unwatched minutes later I pull back, "Wow, that was...wow." He sets me back beside him and wraps his arm around my waist as I rest my head on his chest.

Bridget

"Yes, stab him again! He's not dead yet, girl! NO!" I scream at the screen as Colby laughs at my passion to save the young blonde girl on the screen.

"You know she can't hear you, babe."

I grab a handful of popcorn as I lean forward. "But she should know one stab wound isn't going to work, he has like twelve movies proving he's not an easy kill. See! She drops the knife right beside him, watch, she's going to die now." I lean back confidently and sure enough, the killer gets up and plunges the knife deep into her back several gruesome times. Her screams go unheard because the music at the party was blasting and the kids were drunk or having sex. You can guess who's next to die…duh, the couple having sex.

I nudge him and he turns to me while I stay looking at the screen, "See, he knows to make sure she is dead. She deserved to die."

"What?!" I could hear the shock in his voice.

"Yeah, she was stupid and stupid people die in horror movies." I shrug nonchalantly, my eyes still glued to the screen and he chuckles at my passiveness.

"Man, if we're ever in a horror movie..."

"Babe, if we're ever in a horror movie, you better run! I am taking off my heels and not looking back. Sorry honey, the sacrifice is on you."

He squeezes my hand before kissing me ever so gently, "I'd gladly sacrifice myself for you."

I smile as I take his face in my hand, "My hero! I'll never forget you." We laugh as we continue watching the movie, seeing the slaughter of stupid teens at the end of school year party.

After the movie, we walk around the shopping area just talking.

"So how long have you and Kam been friends?"

"Like forever! She's the only person I trust 100%. She has supported me through the good and bad and vice versa, she's my best friend and my sister. That's why you always see us together, I mean we respect each other's spaces. You won't see her there all the time just when I need her."

He nods, "I admire your relationship and I hope I can come in and add something to your life Nessa, I know that you are very special to me even after only a few days." I want to respond and kiss him like a madwoman, but we are interrupted.

"Hey, Colby!"

Fuck me and all that is holy.

It was that shrill voice that made me instantly feel violent. I have just cause though, for some unknown reason Bridget has always had a chip on her shoulder about Kam. I assume it's because everyone loves Kam while Bridget is known as the town tramp and she is! Whatever sad reason she became that way I do not give one damn, if you dislike the sweetest person in the world, I sure as hell don't care about your ass.

She bounces her hard-fake tits right up to us and turns slightly to block her view of me.

The audacity but I just watch the show.

"Coooolby, you haven't called me to hookup?" She completely ignores me as she grabs his arm and shifts her body close to him, batting her caterpillar ass eyelashes, *does she not have friends? Probably not, she probably slept with all their men.* I squeeze his hand to give him a one and only warning to get rid of her or I will. I can feel Calliope stirring.

"Bridget, you can clearly see I'm on a date right now. Besides, I don't have your number, never have, and don't want it. You can go now..." He removes himself from Bridget's hold as he plants a kiss on my temple and apologizes for her rude interruption, causing a smirk of victory across my face.

Take that you man-stealing slut.

"Hmph, whatever you say, I'm sure I'll be seeing you around. *Nessa*....enjoy while you can."

Oh, this bitch is asking for it.

I slide closer to him and place my hand on his chest, "Oh, believe me, *Bridget*, I have and will continue to enjoy, tonight and every night after that. I suggest you find another victim; you know I have no issue dragging your ass up and down this parking lot. You have yourself a good night! Bye!!!" I maliciously smile and pull Colby towards his car. I can't utter a word, I'm fuming!

He stops me before opening my door and pulls my chin up so our eyes meet. I exhale hard and my face drains of anger, somewhat.

"That gutter slut hates my friend for no reason, so, I don't like her. Simple as that."

He rubs my arms, comforting me, "I get it, just know I never made any plans with her, don't even know why she approached me."

"Oh, I KNOW why...to piss me off. Kam won't let me snatch her up, but I swear if she does one wrong thing, I might go to jail. I'd love to see my fist cracking her slutty jaw."

I huff again feeling that anger rise to the surface, but he grabs me by my neck and plants a fiery kiss throwing me off guard, my whole body relaxes against his as my hands wrap around his neck.

Afterward, I'm all smiles. "Mmm, you always know just what to say. Let's go back to my place." He nods and helps me into the car.

Nightcap

As I open the door to my place, I let him pass so I can lock the door behind him. He lays across my sofa and instantly his eyes close.

"Hey, I do have a bed, there's a whole room dedicated to it actually, come on." I pull him from the couch, and he follows behind me, his arms wrapping around me as he nuzzles into my neck. I feel my temperature rise as his hands roam and caress my body. If he keeps this up, we won't make it to my room, I'll have him take me on the kitchen counter instead.

As we reach my room, I hear a faint squeaking noise. My curiosity piqued knowing it isn't my bed because I'm nowhere near it or even on it. I stop and shush him.

"Shh! Do you hear it? What is that?" We hear it again and again; it sounds like it's not in the room but nearby.

I walk towards my bed, then I lean forward and place my ear to the wall and am shocked when I hear Kam moaning...and John Michael grunting!

OH, MY GODDESS!

"John, please...don't stop..." Kam gasps and then moans into the rocking, which is where the squeaking is coming from.

"Mmm, baby, you feel so good." He answers her desperate pleas.

I gasp and hop off my bed so quickly, shuddering as I step back. "WOW, let's go. The couch IS just as comfortable."

Colby stops me in the middle of my room and smirks, tracing his fingertips along my collarbone and down my arms as he stands behind me, his breath ghosting over my neck. My body is covered in goosebumps and my breath labors. He sees the effect he has on me, "What's wrong, hmm? Uncomfortable hearing your best friend having spectacular sex next door? Listening to him pleasuring her as she cries out in ecstasy. You could be doing the same, I'll have you screaming my name in no time...just say the word..."

I'm stunned almost speechless by his offer and my body screams to let him have me. I notion toward the zipper of my dress. He takes the hint running his hands over the length of my curves causing me to moan slightly. His touch is sending me over the edge.

I let the dress slip off my frame showcasing my new deep burgundy lace balcony bra and boy short set.

He gasps as his mouth starts to water, "Damn, girl." Colby picks me up and falls with my back hitting the bed while he bears his weight on his elbows, placing kisses from my neck to my belly button.

"Mmm, please..." I arch my body upward to meet his as the noise from next door gets more intense. Even I'm impressed and judging by her moans and screams he's doing his job *very* well.

Colby runs a finger down the middle of my back causing me to shiver uncontrollably, bringing my focus back to him. A smirk forms across his face, "Hmm, I'm feeling a bit competitive and I take her screams as a challenge, so challenge accepted."

I don't understand until he is between my legs as I become more and more vocal. He takes delight in my every pant, every whisper, every moan I let out until the sun starts to rise.

After a small nap, he wakes me, kissing my shoulder willing me to open my eyes, but I'm awake the moment he shifts about.

"Good morning beautiful, I think we can say we won that contest last night." I snuggle deeper into his warm muscular body and sigh contently. I finally attempt to get up, but he pulls me back, climbing on top of me, kissing me in between my breasts and I whimper to his closeness. His soft lips press to my supple skin as he teases me.

"Hey, why don't you call them over for breakfast and I'll get it started, okay?" His lips are mere centimeters away from mine and I nod reaching for my phone.

N: Hey, tramp. When you're done screwing John Michael, come over for breakfast. Yes, I heard you. Impressive, we'll talk later! ;)

K: You're one to talk! Oh Colby, don't stop, harder! Ugh... Anyway, we'll be over in ten minutes. Of course, we'll talk, when don't we after a good night of sex? LOL TTYS

I grab my phone and head to the kitchen and my senses are bombarded by the mouthwatering smell of bacon. I take in Colby who is standing in his boxers working on the omelets. He winks as he folds an omelet over after sprinkling it with cheese.

I stand on my tiptoes to kiss his cheek. "Everything smells amazing, who knew such a handsome man could cook so well? You can definitely cook for me anytime." I smile as I reach for the sourdough to make toast, while distracted he takes the opportunity to smack my ass and I yelp while giving him my most seductive gaze, he's really asking for another round but then there's a knock on the door.

Kam and John are still in their pajamas as she smiles at me, I can see the underlying blush as I suspect she knows, I know.

I can't help but take the first jab though, "Morning, tiger or should I say that to John since he's the one who had you screaming his name all night."

I watch Kam grimace and she counters, "I could say the same, even I was curious what positions were used on the other side of that bedroom wall." She winks at me.

That tart! I'll let her have that round.

John shakes his head and walks into the kitchen. He sets the table as I go back to my duty of making the toast. I occasionally watch Kam interact with John; he finds every little way to touch her. It's adorable and I love finally seeing her happy with someone.

Kam always has a positive outlook on life except when it comes to love and with time, I felt she was starting to lose hope. She's always been such a romantic at heart, she deserves the Cinderella fairytale.

After the fourth omelet is done, Colby starts cleaning the pots and pans as I plate all the food and quickly make a small fruit salad. John takes the bowl of fruit and plates putting them on the dining room table. Kam starts to walk away from John, but he pulls her into him, placing sweet kisses on her lips. I'm so caught up watching them I don't see Colby come up behind me as I feel him wrap his arms around me.

"Hey, you."

I giggle, catching Kam's attention.

Just like me, I know Kam is happy seeing me connect with someone, I'm not like her searching for true love, I just like having fun, but for her, it's nice to see me somewhat settled.

We all sit down to breakfast in awkward silence until...

I clap my hands together, "Alright, I'm going to break the ice here, we all heard each other have sex. Usually, Kam is the one suffering from listening to me but surprisingly the tables were turned. So, bravo, John Michael, I don't think I've ever heard her like that before, if ever!" I wink.

I'm barely able to dodge the grape she throws at my head, but I retaliate by hitting her on the cheek with a strawberry.

Kam smirks at me, "Don't start a fight you can't finish, Vanderbilt!"

I hold my hands up in concession, "Alright, no need to waste good food especially since Colby put so much effort into it." I lean over to give him a quick peck and he blushes a bit, gosh, he is so adorable. I see potential in him, he could be something serious.

Yes, I know, I know I have a mate but, in the meantime, I can't date? No harm, no foul, I say.

As we dig in, we idly chit chat. Kam and I finish cleaning the kitchen while the guys settle in on the couch and turn on the tv to find the semi-final round of the soccer tournament, England vs Spain. I drag Kam into my room and close the door, we got some tea to spill.

Day Date

I watch Kam look around the room before turning back to me, *what the hell is she doing?* I raise my brow at her, "What?"

She shifts her weight on her hip, "Knowing you, you had sex everywhere so I'm looking for a safe place to touch. Can I sit on the chair because lord knows..."

If she knew she wouldn't have stepped into my room, period. I laugh internally but remember a safe zone for her. "The chair is safe, that wall you are leaning against... well, we were feeling adventurous. Something primal about being pinned against the wall." I lick my lips as Kam jumps off the wall and shudders to think what happened. She looks behind her cautiously before sitting in my purple chair. I plop on my bed lying in the essence that is Colby and I, he was amazing. I lay on my stomach with a Cheshire grin. I can sense her ears are warming up as the embarrassment grows until she can't take it anymore, she's about to blow so I push just a bit more.

"So...."

Kam remains silent, still staring at me. My smile gets wider and wider...until she finally breaks, "Alright! I had sex with him."

"Obviously...what I want is the down and dirty deets!"

Kam sighs, I know she's dying to spill, I'm her best friend!

"Well, right after you left on your date with Colby, he texted that he missed me and then I said I missed him too and invited him over for a movie..."

"The old Netflix and Chill trick, got it..."

Kam rolls her eyes, "anyway, he came over and we chose a horror movie to watch, but I forgot about that one part where the killer comes up behind her as she's putting on her makeup in the mirror and I screamed and jumped into his lap...and then he kissed me to distract me...and well, one thing led to another. We were on round three by the time you started up your shenanigans, which by the way sounded totally hot. If I weren't completely drained after the fourth round, your sounds could have started the fifth, but he kissed me to sleep until I got your text this morning. All in all, it was amazing, and I don't know Nessa, there could be something there. I'm hopeful, he makes me happy."

Those are the words I want to hear, my best friend is happy, and I'm happy for her.

"So...." Kam looks at me with a telling look, ready for my kiss and tell.

"Well, I guess the tables have turned. Well, as I said, the dress worked perfectly at the movies, he couldn't keep his hands off me. Oh, but get this, as we were leaving someone calls out his name, guess who it is? That slutty skank Bridget, she comes over all giggly and bubbly asking about when he was going to hook up with her, not go on a date or something, just hookup and she says it right in front of me! So, I stay silent to gauge his response, he proceeds to say he doesn't have her number, doesn't want it and that he was on a date with me right now. Oh, you should have seen her face! Anyways, she told me to enjoy it while it lasts and as much as I wanted to punch her in the face, I didn't but the urge was strong. He kissed my temple right in front of her apologizing for the incident and we head back here."

Kam bursts into laughter as I continue this hot mess of an experience, "So we get back and he starts to fall asleep on my couch and I tell him I have a perfectly good bed and drag him towards it until...I heard a squeak and it was driving me crazy that I couldn't find the source until I leaned against the wall and heard you guys. I was all set to sleep on the couch, but he considered that a challenge and - well, you know the rest."

We can't help but burst out laughing at the circumstances. Once we settle back down Kam gasps suddenly, almost scaring me.

"OMG, I just had a great idea! We should double date today, I don't have to open the shop and you're off, we can go to the zoo or..." She looks at me with that look, the look that knows exactly where I've been dying to go! My eyes widen and I jump up like a school child.

"Sample World! Sample World!"

We start squealing before I swing my pillow, starting an old-fashioned pillow fight, jumping up and down on the bed swinging our pillows at each other. The guys hear the commotion and open the door slowly revealing us hopping around and laughing. Their faces were a mix of confusion and…intrigue.

Colby smirks at the sight before him, "You know, this is how most pornos start." John just nods his head, a mischievous glint in his eye.

I throw my pillow as hard as I can at him. "I told you to stop hitting on my best friend, she's not interested in your dirty little three-way."

He shrugs as John pulls Kam into his chest. "Let's go take a shower." He flashes that playboy smile raising his brow and she smiles so wide it must hurt as she agrees. I know what that means!

"Hey! Be back in an hour, you guys! I want to get there when everything's fresh." I flop on my bed pouting and hoping they won't be "showering" too long.

What is happening? I wonder if my best friend is happily attached and having the fun, I've always wanted her to have.

"Penny for your thoughts?" I'm jolted out of my thoughts as Colby sits beside me waiting for me to reply. I sigh a bit, "Nothing really, I'm excited to see her happy, but I'm also worried he might hurt her and then I'll have to turn him into a eunuch and I'm sure that'll put a *slight* damper on our friendship…or I could just kill him and bury his body, either or." I shrug as he hugs me snugly, he smells like our last session and it riles my senses.

"She seems like she knows what she's doing."

"She does but she's also lovesick, searching for her one true love, so she can get preoccupied with that. I want her to find it, the love and whatnot, I just don't want anyone to play with her emotions because I'm the one to take care of her after heartbreak."

His hug comforts me somewhat. "You guys have an amazing friendship just continue to be there...now...we should also get ready." He wiggles his eyebrows as I roll my eyes while I lead him into the bathroom for a steamy shower.

Sample World

An hour later, we head to Sample World, the world's largest sample themed amusement park. A place where you can try delights from all over the world, they even have small fountains filled with various international beverages, you just pay for the cup. I have had my heart set on visiting this place since it opened a year ago about 45 miles from Lovenshire.

We take John's huge lifted truck as Colby's Camaro would have been a tight fit for John. Kam always did like them tall.

As soon as the park comes into view I screech and bounce like a kid hopped up on candy. I can't believe we're finally here!

"There it is! There it is! Sample world, eeeee!" I shake Kam back and forth trying to get her to my level of giddiness. She looks at me like I'm crazy, but I see the spark of excitement in her eyes.

Once parked and taking a picture of the parking area number, the guys help us down from his truck and I drag Kam, full speed, to the ticket counter.

We gaze up at the giant board and stare at all the options as the guys catch up.

Colby and John approach the counter, "Hi, can we get four VIP passes, please?" The clerk rings them up as the guys reach for their wallets.

"Alright, that'll be $240."

"What?!?!" Both of us scream. That is just ridiculous! I could get a four-star hotel for that price and get more than my money's worth.

I pull on Colby's arm to get his attention. "Hey, we could just do general admission. It's just as good." Kam agrees as we hyperventilate at the excessive pricing.

Colby pulls me forward for a gentle kiss, "It sounds like you've been wanting to go for a while so why not do it big for your first time, it's no problem, I want to." I look at Kam who is also getting reassured by John that he wants us to have fun. He places his hand on her cheek, kissing her. His forehead against hers as she smiles and nods.

I look back at Colby, "Thank you! Thank you! Thank you!"

He kisses my forehead, causing goosebumps all over but I have to focus on the deliciousness in front of me, not the one kissing me.

I squeal as I hold my wrist out to get my gold VIP band then after Kam gets hers, I drag her to the first attraction, Appetizer Island. We gaze upon the various displays of every starter food imaginable. I scan the entire selection before I pick my first sample, pretzel bites with beer cheese. That first bite causes me to moan in pleasure as my eyes roll to the back of my head.

"I'd be careful of those moans, sweetheart," Colby interrupts my post-bite orgasm, "I might have to whisk you away for a while. They do have a hotel here."

Confrontation

I considered all my options for response to his statement, should I be a good girl or should she be...Nessa.

D: Let me answer that for you, our mama didn't raise no punk, tease him until he's begging for more! You know who you are!

Dalila was right, that's how I initially met him. I mean I did stick my phone number down his pants, I knew the size of his dick before I knew his name.

Just before I could start my seductive attack, my attention was brought over to the bouncing blonde bimbo approaching, Bridget.

Seriously, What. The. Fuck.

Kam looks at me, I'm just going to sit here and wait for her to say something worthy of a black eye, like any syllable possible. I fake a smile as the never-ending whore approaches.

"Heyyy Colby, nice to see you again and John it's *definitely* good to see you." She bites her lip as she eyes him up and down.

Oh shit!

I swear if you could hear the snap, you would know it was Kam's resolve breaking. She snatches away from John and is within mere inches of Bridget who is smirking smugly, licking her lips as she continues to ogle John over Kam's shoulder. Even I didn't know what to do, Kam was usually never violent, she was my voice of reason.

"Well, hello to you too, Bridget."

Bridget gives her a dirty glance and scoffs, "I don't acknowledge the unimportant."

Kam lets out a struggling sound that was a combination of a laugh and her anger all at once.

I say again…oh…shit.

"Well sweetie, you see when you acknowledged *my* man, it piqued my interest into why the fuck you thought you could, now…I have been MORE than patient with you. For some reason, you don't like me, and I couldn't care less why. But what IS my business is you openly flirting with him thinking because I'm so nice that I wouldn't give you two black eyes and a busted lip for good measure. Won't be so easy sucking dick if your jaw is wired shut now will it?" An evil grin crosses Kam's lips.

Bridget laughs, "Please, Pollyanna, you wouldn't dare!"

Kam steps even closer, her breath fanning over Bridget's lips, "Wanna try me, sweetheart? I fucking dare you."

Even I gasp and try to grab her attention, but instead, John suddenly pulls her back and walks away with her, shouting obscenities until they disappear.

I couldn't help but burst out laughing, I was completely shocked by my best friend's reaction because her having an outburst was rare, nonexistent, really. I turn my attention back to Bridget and scoff, "You know I'll beat your ass for breathing in my direction so, bye-bye gutter slut, come on baby, let's go." I pull Colby behind me to go searching for Kam and John.

I found them in a quiet part of the park. Kam is pacing and talking to herself with John watching her, I shove him away and grab her by the arms. Kam breaks down and the tears start. I hate that she could make her feel this way, she is so much better than that worthless whore.

"Hey, don't you dare give that bitch another thought, she's not worth it."

"Why does she hate me, Nes?! She tries to ruin me, and I-I don't even know what I did to her! She has it out for me! She's vindictive and if she wanted John Michael, she would take him from me!" She croaks out the last part as she lets the tears fall, feeling defeated.

John pulls her into his arms, "Hey, look at me, she will not take me from you. You are smart, beautiful, and the sweetest person I know. She doesn't even compare to you in any way and that's why she's jealous. Please don't let her ruin our day, please?" He kisses her sweetly and she blushes looking him in the eyes, sniffling.

"Come on, beautiful, let's have some fun." He takes her to dessert land to find her favorite dessert, crème brulee, and they found 14 different varieties and she tried them all. He even fed her a couple of bites and kept her smiling and laughing the whole time.

We stuff our faces for the rest of the day then go to Kam's for movie night until Colby almost falls off the couch while nodding off. I just shake my head, "Well that's my cue to get him home. You have to work tomorrow?"

Kam nods, "Let's meet up for lunch, I'm sure we'll have stories." I give her a thumbs up, time for a little fun, he can fall asleep now, but he'll be wide awake soon.

Once the door closes, John lifts Kam's chin so that their eyes meet. He could still feel the tension of the earlier incident. She couldn't hide her distaste of Bridget and her boldness.

"Hey, I meant what I said, you have nothing to worry about." She sighs loudly and grabs his wrist that holds her face.

"You say that now but, though I hate to admit it, she's capable of having any man she wants and if she wants you..." She stops and pulls away. He looks at her starting to withdraw from him and he was not going to have that.

He pulls her into him as he lies back on the couch covering them up in her favorite blanket and kissing her forehead. "I won't let you let her get to you. You are more than enough for me..." He interlaces their fingers and kisses her hand.

"No one should make you feel any less than the beautiful soul that you are. You're the sweetest girl in the world and I'm lucky to have you. Let's make it official, Kamari, I want you to be my girlfriend."

She gasps and turns to face him. "Really? Of course, John!" She wraps him up in a tight hug and then their lips meet fervently.

Meanwhile in my apartment, "Nessa, I want you to be my girlfriend." Colby states matter-of-factly as he holds my hand. *Ohhhh...*

"Absolutely not Colby, I told you I just want to have fun right now. I'm not like Kam. I'm not looking for a commitment of any kind right now, let's just enjoy each other's company." I grab his cheeks forcing a laugh from him.

At the same time, he looks defeated as I continue, "We have the best time and you're an amazing man, I knew that from the moment my hand grazed your dick."

He bursts out laughing, "Wow, you are something else."

I shrug as I sit crisscross on my couch, "I hope I didn't hurt your feelings, I'm just not that girl, yet. Who knows maybe you could change my mind, but I just want to go slow."

I give him the big saucer eyes and he just kisses the tip of my nose. "Of course, sunshine. Now that I'm no longer sleepy and have the sexiest woman in my lap, let's have some fun..."

I hop up and run towards my room squealing as he chases me around my tiny place.

Night at the Bar

Three weeks later, I've managed to persuade Kam to go out to the bar with me for a night of drinking and forgetting the world. It has been challenging as I felt Colby start to withdraw from me after I basically rejected him, I thought being honest would make it okay, but I guess I was wrong. The texts and calls have been less frequent and when we meet up, he is distant. I've decided to surprise him at work tonight in one of my sexiest outfits to assure him of my drop-dead attractiveness towards him and I need Kam as support.

Kam nudges me out of my thoughts, "Oh, I forgot to tell you, I'm meeting John and his friends there, so once you attach to Colby, I won't be alone." I shove her back a little as we use the bathroom mirror to wrap up our makeup.

Kam is in a just below the knee, tight, little black dress. It shows every single dangerous curve she owns, and she's paired it with gold sandals and gold jewelry. My girl is hot to trot! John will surely whisk her away immediately, no way he'll keep her in public like that.

Even I'm shocked at her choice, so I have to tease her a bit. "You finally get some and now you know how to dress? I'm impressed!" Kam rolls her eyes at me and continues to fix her hair and apply her last brush of lip gloss to her perfectly plump lips. She let her beautiful curls fall naturally while putting on his favorite scent for her, lily jasmine.

I decide on a tight red dress that has a split up the side that is dangerously high, I pair it with black heels and a half-up, half-down hairstyle. My makeup screams temptress, but my focus is on Colby, he will not be able to resist me. I need a hot and steamy session once his shift is over; I'm craving it.

I look myself over one more time, oh yeah, I am one sexy siren!

"You ready?" Kam nods and we head out to the bar.

We skip the line as we greet Zeus, the bodyguard. I've always been fond of him; he acts like a dad or a protective older brother. I've annoyed him during prior attendances to no end, but it doesn't stop me from flashing my megawatt smile at him as we approach.

"Zeusy! Nice to see you again."

He cringes, "I told you not to call me that." I reach up to pinch his cheeks, "But you're just so adorable though. Thanks for letting us in, doll!" I blow him a kiss and walk in.

Kam smiles awkwardly as his eyes shift to her; his large frame was quite intimidating. "Thanks." He nods as his eyes follow her as she walks in.

I saunter to the bar, approached by a male waiter that isn't Colby. He isn't bad looking but I'm on a mission.

"Hot damn, beautiful, what can I get you tonight? Perhaps my number? If I can call you, all drinks are on the house." He's still muttering something as I'm looking around for Colby.

"Hey, is Colby working tonight?"

The bartender wipes down the counter, sliding over his number.

"Technically no, he's over there with his fiancée."

Kam gasps and turns around just as I do to see him hugging up on some brunette girl in a short flowy white dress, wearing a sash... and a tiara.... *oh no...*

I feel my heart drop and my pulse race and suddenly the world is moving in slow motion.

"Yeah, they're getting married the day after tomorrow, I think, this is her bachelorette party. I think he's got a party too, but he's so damn wasted he's been groping her all night. I don't think they'll even go anywhere else but home."

I feel my chest rise up and down heavily, there are no tears just yet, but everything is replaying in my head and it just doesn't make sense!

Why did he ask to be exclusive with me if he has a fiancée?! That girl didn't deserve any of the hurt she doesn't even know about, oh, best believe she will though. That bastard isn't going to get away with this, no fucking way!

I think the bartender realized the correlation of my anger and slid a shot my way. I take the shot straight back then I slam down the glass with malice and lean over placing a heavy kiss to his lips, shocking him and Kam. I take his number and slide it down into my red lace bra, giving him a sneak peek. "Thanks, babe I'll definitely give you a call." I wink as I walk over to another part of the bar where we weren't out in the open.

We sit at two bar stools with a high table between us, slightly under the stairs to the upper level.

Kam doesn't know how to play this; she's known me long enough to know when I'm pissed to stay out of my way. But then I feel an emptiness and just sigh. "I'm not feeling the scene. I'm going to go home but you stay! Wait for John Michael and enjoy your time with your boy toy, okay?" I try to sound like I'm okay, but I feel like I'm dying on the inside. This one really hurts.

Kam grabs my hand before I hop off the stool, "Nes, you are worth more than him, he's just another loser who doesn't deserve this beautiful girl I see in front of me. Fuck him, karma will get him one day."

Oh, if she only knew...

I just nod and force a smile, "Thanks, love. Oh, and lover boy just arrived with his friends over there by the entrance."

Sure enough, John and four of his friends had just cleared the entrance and were scanning the crowd, he is obviously looking for his Princess. Before they can take a step further, they are surrounded by girls vying for their chance at one of them.

In the tiny town of Lovenshire, they were the hottest thing around and he is looking exceptionally delectable in his red plaid button-down with the sleeves rolled up to accentuate his muscular arms, he finishes off his rugged look in slightly fitted jeans and boots, a true country boy he was. He's paying no mind to the caravan of girls trying to get his attention once their eyes meet.

Kam stokes the fire by standing up, placing her finger in her mouth and giving her best pout, teasing as he approaches.

"Damn, Princess, you look amazing. Fuck... let's go home I don't want anyone ogling you in this."

He eyes her up and down, biting his lip as he checks out her ass. He immediately groans as he wraps his arm around her, kissing her softly.

"Ready?"

She was about to nod before she catches Colby and his fiancée dancing, looking happy and innocent, not a care in the world like he didn't just ruin her best friend's life and her rage re-emerges. John looks confused until his gaze goes to where she was glaring.

"Excuse me..."

Kam stomps past the dance floor, her heels carrying her quickly reaching the party's private section. Colby's so-called fiancée stops dancing when she sees her approach. As he turns around, Kam swings a mean left hook that leaves him reeling. The fiancée screams as she tries to help him up.

Kam doesn't move, "Karma's a bitch, you pathetic asshole! I hope you're happy! Word of caution honey, your fiancé is a lying, cheating bastard and has been seeing other women. Not me...but I'm the messenger."

Colby stands up with fury in his eyes and it looks like he wants to hit her.

She doesn't flinch. "I fucking dare you..." John steps up quickly with his fists balled. He pushes Kam behind him. A furious John is intimidating and is a good eight inches taller than Colby. "I'll pummel your ass where you stand. Back the fuck up." John's friends join to see about the commotion.

Kam smirks seeing all his big brute friends cornering Colby. She grabs a drink and throws it in his face as the final nail in the coffin, "Enjoy your *marriage*, you spineless jackass. That was for *her*."

She slams down the glass and storms out. She could feel the hot tears of emotion, she knew what she had to do, it was their tradition. John catches up and turns her around, seeing the tears. He hugs her as she shakes her head, over the situation but also frustrated. "I-I need to go to the store, will you take me, please? She needs me." He nods as he wipes her tears with his thumbs.

Sad Song

In the apartment hallway, Kam hears the distinct sound of sad ballads blasting from Nessa's door, knowing she has already progressed so far.

Kam turns to John, "I'm really sorry about tonight but it's tradition to be there when there's a breakup, you don't have to stay, I understand."

She lets go of his hand all set for him to leave but he pulls her into her apartment instead. "Let me get my pajamas, okay?" He, like Nessa, stashed a pair of pajamas in her dresser drawer.

"Okay, besides, I need to find the breakup bourbon" She looks at him as he raises his brow, "yes, it's a thing."

She puts the sadness snacks on the counter as she grabs all the appropriate breakup movies that make you cry. He changes into his pajama bottoms and a black t-shirt while she changes into a black cami/boyshort set.

"Come on, Princess, really? It's bad enough I'm not getting any tonight but that is just torture."

She turns to see him eyeing her choice. She swears for a moment that his eyes turn black but when she looks again, they are his natural baby blue color, must have been a weird light angle. Anyway, she wiggles her butt for good measure, and he groans. She stands still in front of him and places her hands on his chest.

"Now fair warning, this could get ugly. If she kicks you out just stay at my place until I can come back. Oh, and she might take her anger out on you, why? Because you're a man. If you can handle that then grab the two cartons of chocolate chip cookie dough ice cream and the bag of snacks." Kam grabs the bourbon and the movies.

As she locks up her place the distinct sound of Sade could be heard and not much else.

"Not Sade, this is serious. Nessa! Nes, open the door it's me and John."

Delusional

I knew she would come, it's our tradition to comfort one another in our toughest times but I didn't want it, especially if he was with her.

"Go away! I don't want him to see me like this, no one should." I squeak out between my sobs. Kam sighs but then I hear John's voice.

"Nessa please open up, I'll leave once I know you're okay...please Nessa...we brought ice cream."

That'll get you entry into the sad sob fest, brace yourself for the mess that is me.

I click the door, unlock it and walk back to my spot on the couch. Kam opens the door to complete darkness. Her eyes adjust to see me covered in my dark blue mink blanket on the couch. Kam hugs me as I hear John stumble to the kitchen. Kam turns off the pity music and turns on the TV. The glow of the TV revealed what she feared, I have been crying...a lot.

Kam wipes my face, "I brought the breakup bourbon." She gets me to chuckle as she sets the bottle on the table. I want to drown my sorrows in that brown amber liquid. Screw the consequences!

John brings us two bowls of ice cream and sets the other snacks on the table. He gives me a small smile; he really is a sweetheart.

He pulls the DVDs from the bag, "Okay ladies, what movie? Titanic, The Notebook or The Fault in Our Stars?"

I squeeze out a laugh, "Definitely Titanic, it seems to fit best as to how I feel right now." He doesn't answer me, he just hits play.

Kam snuggles up to me as I lean my head against her shoulder while nibbling on my ice cream. John sits in the recliner observing, he is really staring at Kam's ass but now is not the time to be obvious.

"So, tell me what happened after I left." I look at them, I know she didn't just leave without causing a little scene. She may be the sweet one, but I rubbed off on her, I know it, she has a vicious streak especially about those close to her.

John chuckles as he points to Kam, "Oh well, your best friend there completely lost it before we left giving him quite the shiner he'll be sporting for his wedding if he has it at all because the girl heard everything and did not look too happy."

That's my girl!

He opens the potato chips, pouring them into a bowl. "She deserved better, anyway." He adds at the end.

Suddenly there's banging at my door. Loud and annoying I feel Dalila stirring. She wants to make whoever on the other side regret the police knock.

"Nessa! Open up! I'm sorry..."

No fucking way. I must be goddamned delusional to think I hear that bastard's voice on the other side of the door.

He's got some nerve!

Everybody jumps to their feet but only John steps towards the door.

"Let me explain, please! I didn't mean to hurt you just...open the door."

I step in front of John as I put my hand on the knob.

"Umm Kam, what eye did you hit him in?"

"Left eye."

A malicious smirk forms as I feel my vindication coming, "Perfect..." As I swing the door open with my right hand, I swing my left arm hitting my mark and he stumbles back and to the ground.

"Motherfu--!!! What'd you do that for?!" He clutches his eye as he tries to get up off the ground. He leans against the door frame and I step back as John steps closer, just in case.

"What'd I do that for?! Oh, I don't know because you're an inconsiderate prick, a lying, cheating bastard! Vanessa Ann Vanderbilt doesn't cry over some man yet look at me, I shouldn't waste a tear on a pathetic liar like you."

He's still wincing in pain and holding his eye. He sighs and his face falls, I think he finally grasps the brevity of the situation, the guilt all over his face.

He blinks his eye and winces, "Wow, you can really swing a mean left. Nessa, I'm sorry I should have told you about my situation..."

HA!

"You call having a fiancée and an upcoming wedding just a situation? You are something else, not only did I not deserve this, but she sure didn't because she loved you enough to want to spend her life with you. Don't you get how serious marriage is? I may not be looking for it but it's not something I would take lightly."

John practically drags Kam into the kitchen, she's itching to put her two cents in after what happened earlier.

Colby holds his hands out, "I know I messed up, I screwed up badly and I'm so sorry. I realized I'm not ready for that type of commitment and I called off the wedding."

I shift my weight. "Congratulations, why are you *here*?" I raise my brow, crossing my arms, he must know that won't be enough for me to come crawling back.

He reaches for my arm, but I flinch, coming awful close to swinging on him again.

"Because I want to continue to have fun with you...like before."

I laugh in his face as Penelope surfaces and bares her teeth, I'm still in control, but I let Penelope out to instill fear.

"Earth to Colby, you cannot have a wife and a girlfriend! You're lucky there's a human here or I'd let Penelope rip you apart. Not only her but Calliope wants her turn as well and I cannot control her once she is loose." My eyes blacken and Penelope gives a low growl. I let her voice our combined disgust,

"Leave and don't come back. Enjoy your pathetic freedom."

"Nessa please...I... I really care for you. I think I was falling in love with you, Nes I get it now...please give me another chance."

That shocks Penelope enough for me to regain control, I'm also shocked to hear that garbage spew from his mouth. Penelope and Calliope are laughing hysterically, *what a joke*.

"Shove it, Colby you don't know what you want, and you definitely don't know what love is and I can't be with someone so screwed up. You were literally bumping and grinding on her not two hours ago but you're sure you want to be with me now? Not a chance in hell, especially when you made me the other woman. And if you knock on this door once I close it, I'll send John out to handle you because I promise, you don't want either of my girls to finish you off. Have a nice life, Colby."

I slam the door then openly groan. "Bloody hell! Uhhh, why me?! You guys can come back now."

Kam just hugs me and John nods. With his wolf hearing, he had heard the entire conversation; it was a nod of approval.

Briar

"Don't worry, he's just another bump in the road besides, you did get that hot bartender's number tonight, remember? " Kam wiggles her brows before she's pulled into John's lap.

"Eyeing cute bartenders when I'm not around, huh?" He squeezes her sides causing her to yelp.

"Yes...for Nessa. Don't worry I could never leave such a handsome guy; I mean I didn't say anything when you were bombarded by all those girls when you walked in the club tonight."

"Yet I was only interested in finding MY girl..." He kisses her tenderly causing me to gag loudly.

"Spare me you two, I just had a rough night." I slam down two shots of bourbon before filling the glass up again.

"Sorry, babe." I hear Kam whisper to John and he nods kissing her forehead.

"Don't worry about me, let's take care of her." He takes the bottle and pours shots the rest of the night.

Bzzz! Bzzz! Bzzz!

"Oh, bloody pus spewing hell, shut it off!" Kam groans as she finds the nearest thing to throw at the shrill silence killing device. She threw a shot glass in the general direction, but the clanking was worse and something rather large moved underneath her. She was laying on something warm, hard, and quite muscular. She moves the pillow to see a smiling and half-naked John Michael.

"Morning, Princess."

His morning voice was so sexy, but it was, "Too loud, baby. Morning."

She whispers, finding the bourbon bottle 3/4 empty.

She groans, "How many shots did I have?" She rolls off him and sits up holding her head.

He shifts to sitting up and stretches, "Last I remember Nessa had four, I had six, and you, my little minx, had seven. You just had to prove that you weren't a lightweight but then you passed out right after, well actually, you tried to get into my pants first then you passed out." He chuckles remembering how she promised to give him the best blow job of his life before she fell asleep in his arms.

"Well, did I get into them?" She smirks as she licks her lips.

He scoffs, "Honey, I'm not that type of guy." She laughs rolling her eyes.

She looks for Nessa on the floor, "Is she in her room?" She stands up to go check on her, but he pulls her back into his lap wrapping his big, strong arms around her delicate frame, she had to suppress the moan threatening to escape.

"Yeah, they're in there, I wouldn't bother them."

She instantly sobers up and is immediately irritated. "*They*? Please tell me she didn't forgive that asshole?!"

He shakes his head and smiles, "Nah, apparently he's that irresistible bartender you guys were drooling over." His response dripped in jealousy.

She tries to soothe him and straddles his lap, "Aww, somebody sounds jealous. Don't worry, buttercup, you're the only one I want." She smiles while wrapping her arms around him, kissing his cheek as he squeezes her ass.

"Did you just call me buttercup?" She nods, "Are we not in the cute pet name stage? You call me Princess, so I had to think of something cute."

They find comfort in each other and are so close to falling back asleep when the door opens and I walk out giggling with nothing but a large button-up on, *his* button-up.

My rebound stood about six foot two, a bit shorter than John, he had dark brown hair that was pulled into a bun, his skin is tan, like been on the beach tan, covered in tattoos, and he had the most perfect smile. Let's not get into the night of unbridled passion he gave me that made me forget…what's his name.

Kam snaps back into reality when she feels the fingers of her boyfriend tapping on her leg. She has obviously been staring, possibly drooling.

"Don't you start! Only you, buttercup." She gives him a few quick kisses and hugs him tight.

Oh brother, "If you two could stop being so adorable I want you to meet Briar, Briar this is my best friend Kam and her boyfriend John Michael." He gives a quick wave before he settles in the kitchen, "Hope you guys are hungry for a big breakfast." He starts milling around gathering everything he needs as Kam takes me aside.

"Umm, when did this little tryst happen?"

"Oh, around your 5th or 6th shot, you said I should give him a call, that I needed to release my frustration with some angry sex, so I called, and he had just gotten off his shift. He came by with chocolates to apologize for spilling the beans earlier. You, missy, were two shots from being completely naked and attacking John Michael, so I took Briar into my room...and well, you know things happen. He might be the best one yet and besides, I hadn't slept with Colby in two weeks."

"So... are you two?"

I wrap my arm around her and shake my head while smiling, "We're just friends Kammi Bear, besides, I just got over whatever that was with Colby."

She agrees, "But don't you think it'll be weird because they work together?"

A devilish grin crosses my face, "I think it'll be fun visiting Briar at work." I wink and walk back into the kitchen leaving her to John's relentless kisses. Briar's just finishing up the waffle batter as John comes in to cook the bacon and eggs. We set the table while the guys finish up the cooking. Can't say that it isn't hot watching them cook for us, it's a complete and utter turn on.

After breakfast, Kam and John head back to her place. Briar stands at my door holding my hand. "I'm really glad you called me, I'm not glad of the circumstances but I hope you look to me for more than just a rebound, you're a beautiful girl, Nessa. Let's hangout sometime, okay?"

He kisses my forehead and I can't help but blush a little. "Absolutely, thank you for the much-needed stress relief."

We share a laugh, if he makes me remember another minute of last night he won't leave this apartment for another four hours. "Anything for you, gorgeous especially if I get to look forward to doing that thing again." Now we're both blushing, it's no secret I can be quite wild in bed but add bourbon to the equation and you've unlocked Pandora's Box.

He places a kiss to my forehead, then nose, and finally on my lips. "See ya later, gorgeous." I smile as I close the door.

I went back to my bedroom to get my outfit for the day, but then I notice a note:

I have never seen such a determined girl or a sexier one, that red dress had me instantly. I want to get to know the girl I met at the bar, but I also want to meet her sweet and caring side, her gentle side, the one who cries at sappy love movies. I hope tonight wasn't a one-time thing, let me take you out tomorrow. Just the two of us. You're special Nessa, I hope you know that. Briar.

I grin while tapping the paper against my hand, "Perhaps Briar, but first I have some unfinished business to attend to." I look over in the corner and laugh before heading into the bathroom for a much-needed shower. I had worked up quite the sweat during last night's marathon romp.

Sweet Revenge

In the dark of night, I park my car a block away from Colby's address, possibly the house he still shared with his fiancée. I pull my mini cart from the trunk and load it with cans and slowly make my way towards the home. For dramatics I dressed in all black with a ski mask on to conceal everything but my eyes, but truth be told I didn't give a damn if anyone saw.

Ahhh…there it was.

His precious Camaro, the one that would shatter him to pieces…if something… were to happen to it…

I walk slowly so my supplies don't rattle. I notice all the lights are off in the house, good, maybe they are already asleep. I pull the cart right next to the car and brandish my trusty flat head screwdriver.

I pause for a moment, *was I really about to do this? Was I just petty enough to exact revenge?* Then I thought about all the lying and cheating he did, it's okay if his fiancée forgives him but not me. He is going to pay for his deceit.

I place the tip of the screwdriver between the can and the lip and press upward to relieve the lip from the can. I do the same for the remaining four cans, grinning at the fluorescent green goo that shown even in the dead of night. He would get the message night or day.

I prop the first can on the edge of his driver's side door going for the kill immediately, pouring the fluorescent message all over his interior, the lime justice splashing over every detail of his classic car. I even open the glove compartment and middle console to fill them up. If I had thought about it longer, I would have filled his trunk.

After feeling some retribution, I use the remaining four cans to evenly and professionally coat the exterior. I am satisfied with my work but need one last kick to the nuts, so I scrawl "cheater" with the screwdriver on top of the hood in huge letters and the paint covers that little surprise for later. I take a few photos and of course my signature selfie, whistling happily as I head back to my car.

I take the scenic route home to enjoy my victory. I finally get home, park my car and come up the stairs still whistling. *Man. Life is good…*

Before I can fully enjoy my stunt, I'm pulled into Kam's apartment where John and his friends are waiting.

Kam looks like she has been worried sick. "Girl have you completely lost it?! Colby has been calling nonstop looking for you, what did you do? He threatened me so I had John come over, he is irate!"

I toss my paint-splattered gloves and mask to the ground by the door and sit down as if nothing happened. I can't play the innocent card like Kam, but I can try.

"You're staying here with us until he calms down, I don't trust him." She paces the living room a bit frantic.

I huff, "If he knows what's good for him, it's him who better stay back, I can very well take care of myself." I look at the guys and they nod but must play the role to not seem suspicious.

"Are you mad, woman?! He sounded very threatening like he would physically harm you, I can't let anything happen to you, just please...stay here."

Kam is obviously very worried, so I sigh, "Fine. Looks like a ridiculously hot sleepover, anyway. How could a girl say no?" I take in all the delicious males in the room, nobody I would bang but nice to look at. I couldn't help but burst into a fit of laughter.

Kam just shakes her head and there's silence for a while until she couldn't hold it. "Okay, I'm dying to know, what did you do?! I know you took pictures."

I perch myself on the couch and pull out my phone, everyone crowds around me in anticipation. I click on my photo gallery and there is Colby's lime green dream in all its glory.

Everyone gasps, I heard a few curses. "Nes, not his Camaro! He's never going to get that out." Kam laughs as I go through the photos.

"Damn, Nessa, the middle console?"

"And the glove compartment too, John. But that's not the coup de grace, I keyed 'cheater' on the hood, but the paint covered it...sort of a part two."

All the guys groan, it's known that every man's fear is for their car to fall victim to a vindictive girl, but I say the simple solution is…don't screw up! Shocking!

Satisfied, I close my phone, "And now I can move on. So, did we order food or not? I worked up quite the appetite."

John points to the counter where three pizza boxes were, and I happily jump up to snag a slice of pepperoni. I take a bite and it's orgasmic, I remove my top, revealing my pink lace bra. I needed to change clothes badly.

"Hey, do I still have pj's here? I'm going to change." I throw my shirt over my shoulder. Me and my pizza head into Kam's room.

The Aftermath

Kam turns to see all the guys with their mouths open including John. She clears her throat giving him a questionable look. He doesn't hear her as he talks to the guys.

Oh, okay.

She pulls her tank top down to showcase the lace of her red bra, a stark contrast to her black cami. She ties it into a crop top and pulls her shorts up slightly making them cheeky as she gets up, passes in front of the group, and goes to grab something to drink.

John's jaw drops further watching her walk to the kitchen but when she turns around to grab the water from the bottom drawer of the fridge, he almost loses it.

"Hot damn, John, your girl is freaking gorgeous and that body..." His buddy bites his lip while they all nod in agreement. The same way they were looking at Nessa, they were now looking at Kam.

"Hey, eyes front, that one is mine! Don't you have a movie to watch?" His eyes go black as an emphasis to his statement and his buddies turn around.

He gets up as she reaches for the top shelf to grab the popcorn, accentuating everything. He comes up behind her and grabs it for her, she doesn't say anything as she opens the bag tossing it in the microwave.

"Princess..."

He waits for her to acknowledge him. She turns and crosses her arms further accentuating her breasts. He gets distracted for a second before his focus is back on her.

"What, John Michael?"

Not babe, honey, or even buttercup.

He pulls her to him, hugging her and kissing her forehead while reaching for the hem of her shorts pulling them down.

"Okay I get it, I shouldn't have been staring like that, I'm sorry I was caught off guard. But can we put MY girls away?"

The microwave beeps breaking the tension and she bends down to grab a bowl. She stands up but doesn't pull her shirt down. She empties the bag in the bowl then hands it over to the guys before returning to the kitchen for her water, not even looking him in the eye before she goes to her room slamming the door, startling everyone.

I jump when Kam slams the door, "Whoa! What the hell, Kam? What's wrong?" *This can't be good.*

Kam plops down on her bed and shrugs her shoulders, fearing she might get emotional.

I already feel the dam is about to burst.

"Come on, what is it?" I watch her because I know she's upset but she doesn't want to seem whiny or needy.

She sniffles a bit, "Did you have to take your shirt off in front of them?"

I realize my mistake and I kneel in front of her. "Oh, Kammi I'm sorry, it wasn't on purpose you know I just feel like I'm at home here, I didn't think about it. I'm really sorry."

Kam rolls her eyes and sighs, "Maybe I am just overreacting."

I look her over and pop her bra strap, "Trying to prove a point I see, nice bra though." I pull her tank down to see the whole thing, nice.

Kam squeals "Thank goodness we're not the same size."

Just then there was a soft knock, "Princess, please talk to me."

She sighs heavily while looking to me for support.

I shake my head, "Oh no, you need to fix this right now."

I go to open the door and come face to face to a sad-looking John whose eyes land on hers. I went to join the guys watching some action movie where they were yelling at the main character to do something. Guys love violence but I do, too!

John closes the door behind him and sits in front of her on the floor laying his head in her lap.

"I'm sorry, princess."

Her heart melts seeing him so apologetic and she feels bad for how she reacted. She kisses his cheek, "No, I'm sorry I shouldn't have reacted like that, it was stupid. I'm just...scared to lose you and I let my insecurities get to me."

He turns to face her now. "Look at me, if I need to tell you every day I will, but you mean the world to me, Kam. You don't need to worry, you're my girl." She laughs pulling him into a hug and kiss. The kiss escalates and they break away briefly catching their breath.

"You think they'll notice if we..."

"They probably already think we're having sex."

He smirks, "Well, then let's prove them right!"

She screams getting away from him. He stalks her until she is pushed up against the door. With nowhere to go, she just watches his every movement until he's practically on top of her.

"Hey."

"Hi."

He leans in closer, mere centimeters away from his prize until there's a loud banging and then yelling.

Nothing to Talk About

I swear I'm about sick of people banging at the damn door. Whoever this is, is about to feel my wrath! I swing the door open and come face to face with a livid Colby.

"What the fuck is wrong with you?! You totaled my car!"

"You lying cheating bastard, you thought I would let this shit go?! You got a lot of nerve being mad when you ruined my life with your lies!"

I notice Kam and John walk out as I'm screaming at Colby who looks beyond pissed.

"You deserved it, you jackass! Your little fiancée may be dumb enough to forgive you but I'm not. I don't care if you report me, the sheriff is my uncle. Now I'm not going to say this again, go away and don't come back!"

Calliope is persuading Penelope to let her scratch the surface. I almost let her too, but Kam is present.

We are interrupted by a light knock that breaks the tension, but it doesn't break my gaze. Kam opens the door to reveal, "Briar, hey." Thank the Moon Goddess I was about to have John escort Kam out and reign hell as Calliope. I was that pissed.

Briar looks at Kam giving her a little smile, "Hey Kam, I thought I heard Nessa's voice, is she here?" She nods as she opens the door further and all eyes are now on him. He focuses on me which he notices my eyes are brimmed in tears, they were angry tears, I was done being hurt.

He reaches for me, "Nessa, baby, are you okay? I could hear you screaming from the hallway." He pulls me into his strong manly chest and his scent is comforting. I finally sigh in relief, until I hear a loud scoff behind me.

"Him?! Really Nessa, way to aim low."

Wow.

His words sting but I try not to feel the pain he wants me to, after all, he has no right to judge, at all. My breath hitches as Briar steps in front of me, his stance is protective.

"Oh really, Colby? At least I'm not hiding a fiancée in my back pocket or the fact that you were getting married in two days and still trying to sleep around. At least with me, she doesn't have to worry about me hiding a family. You screwed up by starting something in the first place, talk about aiming low, you're a scumbag, did they know you've done this before...several times? It was Dani then there was Trina before that, right? We should all feel sorry for Christine because she doesn't deserve to marry a prick like you."

I step in between them, "Don't worry about him, Briar, he's not worth your breath. I've said my piece and had my revenge so now I'm moving on."

He smiles, kissing my forehead, I feel the warmth in my core. "Yeah, she's with me and if you don't want any more trouble with your fiancée or her dad, who owns the bar, I suggest when you see her you look the other way. Got it?"

The entire room is silent as everyone watches the exchange, the tension thick.

Colby sighs and runs his hand over his face, "I'm sorry Nessa, I really am, I should have been honest and allowed you the chance to decide but you were so sexy, that smile, and that dress, I just couldn't help myself. In the little time I've known you, you've made a big impact, I saw everything differently with you around. I guess you made me realize that I'm not ready yet. This whole thing has been quite the eye-opener."

Kam bursts out laughing with John and I'm right behind them. She waves her hand, "I'm sorry, it's just...eye...opener! HAHAHA!!!!" She points at her eye referring to his still healing one.

He shrugs his shoulders and chuckles, "Yeah, thanks ladies for the memories, I'll never forget you." He turns around and exits the apartment.

Party Time

Once he's gone all the tension in the room dissipates, Briar wraps me up in a tight hug. I look up at him and bite my lip.

"I'm sorry, you didn't have to interfere in our fight but thank you for being there."

He shrugs, tightening his grip. "No problem, I actually came by because you never answered me about our date, so what do you say?"

I kiss him ever so sweetly, "How can I say no to my hero? Absolutely, tomorrow night but since you're already here...let's go to my place. I need someone to…cuddle with."

I look at Kam who has that knowing look. "Shut up." I mouth 'Don't judge me' and Kam holds her hands up in defeat. I drag Briar out and to my place, it is time to release some stress and I have the perfect patient to play sexy nurse with. I know Kam can hold her own tonight.

When Kam turns back around, she's faced with five handsomely rugged men to include her own. If she were that type of girl...

"Thanks, guys, you don't have to stay." John notions at the door and they bid them a goodnight. He shuts the door behind them, turning around with a wicked grin.

"I do believe I have some making up to do, don't I, Princess?" He licks his lips slowly. She matches his steps but in the opposite direction to avoid him. She squeals but no one can help her as she makes a run for her bedroom, but he slides in before she can close the door.

"Ahhh!"

She is surprised by his quickness. He cages her against the door, hands on either side of her head.

"Oh, you thought you could get away, there's nowhere to go and you've been wearing that sexy little number all night, teasing me. Now I want time with my girl."

She seals the deal, "Please."

After having my way with Briar, I hop out of the shower, wrapping my body in an oversized towel, my hair left out to air dry. When I step out of the bathroom, he is lying on my bed in nothing but his boxers. I can't help but lick my lips at the sight of all his tattoos, his entire chest was covered and a half sleeve on his arm. He even has one adorning his calf adding to his incredible sexiness.

"Come here, doll face."

Ooh, the way he orders me around!

I blush slightly as I lay next to him in my towel but rest my leg and arm across him, dragging my fingertips in lazy circles. He kisses my forehead before chuckling.

"What an interesting night."

I laugh, "You can say that again! I'm so over the drama...please tell me you don't have a wife, love child, or a locked-up sibling in your attic?" I look at him with seriousness. He laughs but then realizes I'm not joking.

"Oh, you're dead serious. No, doll, I don't have anything like that you can even come to my apartment. I may even let you peek at my sex dungeon."

I lick my lips; my imagination is running wild. "Ooh a sex dungeon, how did I get so lucky?"

Three months later...

Everything has gone seemingly back to normal. I beat loudly on my bedroom wall, "Twenty minutes, Kam!" I can hear her squealing and giggling no doubt the workings of John Michael. I climb off my bed and head to my bathroom to finish my makeup. I'm wearing a leopard print wrap dress and high heels, contrasted with light but sexy makeup.

There was a knock at my door, I skip my way over to answer it, "Hey, Bri." He kisses my cheek handing me a single red rose.

"Hey gorgeous, you look amazing, ready for a night of fun? I bet you'll have no problem finding someone to take home in that!" He spins me causing me to giggle as I try not to fall out of my heels. He pulls me into him and smiles, giving me a tender kiss on the cheek.

It has been a few weeks since I realized that Briar is bi and that we are better as great friends than a couple. We still fool around but it is obvious that he is attracted more to men. He surprised me when he told me that I was the only female that interested him enough to sleep with.

I put the flower in a vase, "Thanks sunshine, you always make me feel special even though I know you'd rather be under Tomlin's fine ass right now, maybe he'll be at the party. That would be your best chance to bag him."

Briar sighs, his face fell a bit, "I don't know Nes, are you even sure he's bi or even curious? He's super hot and I don't want to make a fool out of myself. Especially in front of the whole town!"

I survey his outfit; he's wearing tight blue jeans and a red Henley with the sleeves rolled up. There is something sexy about a guy who rolls up his sleeves, I don't know what it is. I think it screams he's about to get down to business and it's going to get dirty. I find myself licking my lips before I shake my head to come back to the present and smile wickedly.

"Oh, you look too hot to be ignored, we'll tag team and get him alone to see. Tonight just may be your lucky night!" He blushes wildly.

"Enough about me, what about you? Anyone in particular on your radar?"

I turn to look in the mirror looking myself over once more. "Nah, just need to have fun and the yearly bonfire party is tradition. Besides, after being around Kam and John kind of leaves me wanting more than just casual sex. Don't get me wrong I'll still have that too, that's what I got you for, but I get what Kam wants, that everlasting love. Ugh, she's turning me into a love sap! Let's grab the lovebirds and go."

I knock on her door and Kam answers very quickly. She's in a summer wrap dress and sandals. I look behind her, "I thought John was with you? Wait, why were you giggling?"

She laughs, "I was on the phone with him, he's already there with his friends and he is wasted. He said he was going to take me into the nearest bedroom and have his way with me."

Briar and I start to giggle like schoolgirls as we rush her out of her place. "Well, let's get you laid then!"

Caught

We drove out into the thickest part of the forest to Aaron Virgil's country estate. He always hosts the town's yearly celebration with a bonfire and huge party on his massive amount of land. By the time we arrive, the fire is roaring, people are dancing around it, and roasting marshmallows. The music is blasting over the five acres of land. Each of us is handed a welcome beer at the gate as we enter.

Briar and I go searching for the bar to order some shots then we dance and twirl by the bonfire. We sing loudly to the music as we shoot back the shot and chase it with the beer. I'm really feeling it now, let the fun begin! Kam seems to be feeling too good and now she needs her man in more ways than one.

I'm grinding on some guy sitting on a haystack near the fire as Briar takes in the surroundings sipping another beer, seemingly keeping his eye out for Tomlin, he is on a mission.

Kam walks up the stairs of the main house into another full-blown party, a party within the party. Inside the music was rock and plenty of drinking games were going on at once. Someone hands her another shot to which she happily takes.

She accidentally bumps into one of John's friends. "Kaaaaam, h-how are you, gorgeous? Come here and give me a hug!" She's painfully pressed up against Tyler before she can respond.

"Ty! Ty put me down! It's good to see you too, where is John?" He tries to hand her a shot, but she declines.

"Oh, I lost him a while back he was talking to...what's her name...Bridget! Yeah her and then they disappeared somewhere." He shrugs his shoulders knocking back the shot she refused, unaware of the turmoil he just caused.

Her stomach sinks and she has sobered up at the revelation. She tries to not show her worry but then again Tyler is too drunk to notice as he cheers for his buddies playing beer pong.

Kam heads upstairs, her feet feel like cement she has to drag to find out the truth for herself. Every second feels like hours and now she is feeling completely unnerved.

She opens the first door to a very busy couple and she shuts the door immediately. "Sorry!" She had to have invented a new shade of red after that discovery.

She chuckles before opening the next door, occupied bathroom. No wonder there was a line for the other one. *Was everybody getting some?*

She checks one side and starts at the other to which she finds a guy arguing on the phone, who tries to throw something at her to shut the door...*rude!*

She is a bit appalled but shrugs it off. She feels mother nature calling but her curiosity is calling more, and bodily functions will just have to wait. She hears a voice in her head tell her to keep searching, that she will find the answer she is seeking.

Must be my conscious, she thought. Weird, she never heard it as loud as she just did.

I Warned YOU

Before she can touch the knob of the door, she hears moaning, a deep male moaning, and some other sound she couldn't quite figure out.

Instead of barging in, she listens closely against the door. There it is again, a guy moaning and now a girl giggling.

"I know she can't do it as good as me, in fact, *we* know she can't. She's such an annoying goody two shoes, I can act out any dirty fantasy you could possibly ever want."

Again, she hears the sound she can't make out followed by more moans.

"Damn girl, you're so good at that, she is too innocent to do that, but you can be my dirty girl, right? Whatever I want, right? She doesn't have to know."

"Mmm, whatever you want, John. I'll be your dirty little secret. You taste so good, baby."

They share a laugh as Kam's heart breaks behind the door. She turns the knob slowly so they don't hear the tumbler click and it opens slowly and there, in the middle of the room is John with his pants at his ankles, his eyes closed and hand on Bridget's head as she does what she does best on her knees. That is the noise she heard, that dirty slut sucking off her man.

They only notice after Kam gasps. She is met by a devilish smirk from Bridget as she wipes her mouth, the saliva of her exploits still dripping from her chin. She still had him wrapped around her fingers but then gets up and kisses John square on the lips. He doesn't fight her on it either, he's turned but Bridget's eyes are honed on Kam's, she is tasting sweet victory and being caught for her is a bonus.

John is slow to react, either it's the shock or the copious amount of liquor he consumed beforehand his reaction is delayed but hers isn't as she walks away at breakneck speed.

I'm headed to the bathroom to empty my bladder of all the shots I took when Kam nearly pushed me over as she ran down the stairs…was she crying?!

I can't react quick enough because she is already out of my sight, but I suddenly feel a wave of rage. And from what I can tell it is justified.

D: *Hey, she came from that open room, let's go see.*

I walk into the room to see Bridget kissing John as he buckles his pants.

Oh. Hell. No. Did he not understand what the fuck I told him?

I gave all my rage and anger to *her*, he was about to meet her, and it wasn't going to be pretty and you know what, this fucker deserves it.

My eyes turn icy gray as a gust of wind sweeps through the hallway, the force of the wind whipping my hair all around. The people in line for the restroom immediately vacate the area.

Calliope steps forward and blocks the entrance.

"You stupid bastard, I told you not to hurt her and here you are with that filthy town whore!"

Bridget approaches me but that is a big mistake on her part. Calliope brutally slams her into the wall with a flick of her hand before she utters a peep.

"No one asked you, bitch, I'll deal with you later but you...I specifically told you not to hurt her, that she was fucking special and yet here we are! I ought to castrate you where you stand but from what I just saw there wasn't much there, to begin with. Kam's screams and moans look like she was being pretty...generous." I eye him up and down begging for him to say something stupid.

It seems like my tirade brought him back to the present and he sobered up enough to gain some sense of the entire situation.

"Shit! What did I do? I was drunk and I-I don't know...she was telling me all the things I wanted to hear and before I knew it she was on her knees...I didn't mean to, Nessa you got to believe me! I need to find her, I-I really screwed up! I can't lose her, please!"

I cup my hand making him grasp his throat fighting for air as he drops to his knees.

"Oh John, Nessa's not in control and yeah, you fucked up. I will not let you try to make this make sense because it doesn't. Don't you remember you even spoke with Kam before saying you were going to take her when she got here so I call bullshit on your pathetic little excuse. You didn't care, you're an asshole and you screwed up. And mark my words this isn't over, I'm going to make every effort to ruin your life, to make it a living hell."

I look over and Bridget is on her feet again but not for long. I regain control from Calliope and swing a mean right hook connecting with her nose and when she's down I punt her, like a football, in the stomach for good measure.

I crouch down to a painfully wheezing Bridget, "And you, you trifling, dirty whore, watch your back...at ALL times. I know several places to hide your heavily used body."

Bridget can only cough, still gasping for air. I can just finish her now, but I want her living in fear and my best friend's well-being is much more important right now.

Tears

I run out of the house after I link a few people to see if they saw where Kam went. Someone said she was headed to the lake out back.

Once again, I would be the one to put her shattered pieces back together. My sweet girl has such a big heart, and this was going to take a while to get over, but I will be there every step.

I trudge through the forest path until it opens to a clearing. I see her back heaving as she lets her emotions out; she doesn't even bother to react when I step on a twig and it snaps.

"I hope this is a horror movie where the murderer comes to end this feeling of pain."

I immediately sit and hold my best friend. "Don't say that, you are better than him! I will make him pay, Kam. I'll make his life a living hell. He just wasn't your one and you know what, I'm glad. Your happy ending is coming. Come on, let's go home and pig out on junk food and watch whatever you want."

Kam looks at me, tears streaming down her face, "Why am I never good enough?"

I feel the lump in my throat, I want nothing more than to cry at that hurtful statement, but I am here to comfort her.

"Stop it right now, you are more than enough, it's them who don't meet your standard. You are the golden ticket to true love and happiness; you just haven't found him yet but he's there. I know it, I learn from you every day that love is a precious commodity we shouldn't take for granted."

She takes my hand and we call for a cab to take us home. I tell Briar to stay and have fun, that this was our tradition and I would text him later. He agrees but not before giving Kam a strong hug. He places his hands on her face, so she is looking at him.

"Hey, you are gorgeous, doll. The time I've gotten to know you only solidifies that you are a rare and precious gem no ordinary man can hold. You cry it all out and then get back to you, a beautiful, strong, caring woman. Remember you always have me." They share a quick laugh before her face falls back to reality.

"Thank you Bri, you're the best." He nods as he kisses her forehead.

He turns to me and whispers angrily, "The first thing I'm going to do is kick that asshole in the nuts, maybe a few times. I'll let you know what happens." I just laugh hysterically.

Once we get home, Kam slumps on her couch staring into nothing as she grabs a pillow to hug. I turn on the kitchen light behind her to make some popcorn. Kam gets up and goes to her room to change. She comes back out in pajamas before wrapping up in her blanket, still gazing into nothingness.

I sit beside her, "Hey, what movie do you want to watch?"

I can see her lip quiver on the verge of another breakdown, but she holds back. "T-the Color Purple." I start the movie and head back into the kitchen grabbing the breakup bourbon.

I set down the bottle and go to grab the shot glasses that I forgot. I come back to see Kam turning up the bottle gulping down a large amount before I can snatch it from her. I look at her in shock but also pity because her eyes are full of tears.

"I don't want to feel like this anymore."

She leans over and lays down against the armrest.

"I know but drinking yourself to death isn't the answer. You've had enough for tonight just lie there I'll bring you something to eat." I place the popcorn bowl close while I throw the loaded fries in the oven. After the amount she drank she's going to need carbs to soak it up. She is definitely going to regret that tomorrow.

I sit back down, and Kam switches over to lay across my lap.

"Nes?"

She looks up at me. "Hmm?"

Kam sighs and looks back at the television. "I don't think true love exists, maybe there are no such things as soulmates. Maybe I am destined to be alone because apparently according to them I'm too 'goody goody' to do the things she would do."

Just thinking about what I saw had Calliope whispering to Penelope, obviously plotting a world full of pain.

"Don't you dare listen to a damn word they say and never, I mean never compare yourself to a whore! I should have never let him get this far; he isn't worth your tears. I can't wait for you to meet your one and when you do, you'll realize you would have only been wasting time with John Michael. Focus on all the things that make you great, he knows he screwed up already, now show him why."

She nods as she goes silent, taking her contemplation inward.

The next morning Kam wakes up in her bed wondering how she got there until she hits me in the face, waking me up out of a decently dirty dream.

"Owww! Son of a... what gives?!" I hold my hand over my eye trying to blink the pain away.

"Sorry...how did you even get me in here?"

I sat up a bit while still holding my face.

"Well after you drank a quarter of the bottle and then consumed all the fries in sadness you ran to the bathroom to empty your stomach not an hour later and instead of walking back, you plopped down in bed. Let me be honest and tell you that you didn't quite entirely make the toilet 100% and I had to clean up. You owe me big time!" I shudder to think about it.

"Sorry... I can't explain how I felt I just wanted to feel something other than heartache, but this hangover proves I don't want to feel that either. What's worse is now people are going to talk and if it's not already it'll be all over town!"

"That's his burden to bear, not yours! He'll have to deal with why such an amazing girl isn't with him anymore. I hope it makes him miserable. And besides getting caught with the town tramp isn't a mark of honor, it's desperation."

Hello, Kayden

Three hours later, I make an excuse to get out as I make a beeline for the packhouse, I have a plan and I have intel from before this shitshow happened and he isn't going to get away with this.

I storm in and run smack dab into Kayd while trying to get to Alpha Mitchell's office.

"Oof...Sorry about that, Vanderbilt it was my..." Kayd stops and sniffs around me, here we go...

"I swear it is the most intoxicating scent when you come around. I really should meet this friend of yours."

I wave my hand trying to get him out of my path of destruction. "Not now Miller, I am here to make someone pay for hurting my best friend, now either help me or get out of my way! I seek vengeance and I am damn sure going to get it!"

He holds his hands up, "You know since my dad will be transitioning the pack over real soon, I am starting to handle issues for him that don't involve other Alphas. Tell me what this problem is…"

I take a deep breath to calm my nerves and my girls, "Not what but who..."

We sit down in the living room and I tell him everything that happened. His facial expression says it all, "Wow talk about an idiot, to mess with someone who sounds so sweet and kind, possibly the perfect woman. Well, what do you want me to do?"

"I want him gone because of not only that but I also heard that he was in contact with a rogue from the north pack, I want it investigated and if it is true I want him exiled from our pack! If I can't rip him apart, I don't want to see his lying, cheating face!"

Kayd nods in agreement, I see him cower a bit toward my rage though I'd never disrespect the next Alpha in line, I'm just so angry.

"We have been following intel on John for some time and the rumors are indeed true, we were trying to gather more but I think I already have enough to convince my father. I'll talk to him ASAP about it and I'm sorry about your friend...maybe you could bring her to the packhouse so..."

I immediately hold my hand up to stop him, "She's human, Miller...besides, she just had her heart broken by that bastard. She won't be ready for anything, not even our big bad Alpha to be."

I wink and he chuckles as I walk out satisfied, soon I will have my revenge.

A week later Kayd calls me back to the packhouse. As I approach he does his usual and I sigh, "I know, I know I smell wonderful, like morning sunrises or whatever, blah blah blah...what do you have for me, Miller?" He laughs as we walk into his office. He sits down and clasps his hands together.

"Well, Vanderbilt, he was indeed talking to the north rogue pack and plotting to help them infiltrate and try to overthrow my dad and me. He is now an enemy to the Cheshire pack and banned from pack grounds. He was instructed that he had three weeks to leave town or he would be chained in the dungeon and tortured. I hope that information makes your friend happy."

He gives me a small smile that I return, "Well, I can't tell her about the chaining and torturing, but it'll be good to know that he'll be leaving so she can move on in peace. He doesn't even deserve that; he deserves to be ripped in half and fed to the dogs. Bastard." Kayd looks at me, shocked by my response.

I switch the subject of our conversation to something more somber; I reach for his hand and squeeze it gently.

"Hey, how are you holding up? You know your dad was a wonderful Alpha and I know he's up there bragging about how you'll continue his legacy keeping us as the strongest pack."

Kayd sighs heavily, it wasn't too long ago that he buried his dad after a sudden heart attack. They had his service just yesterday.

"It's still pretty fresh, I'm just worried about my mom and I pray that the bond break doesn't kill her. I don't know what I would do if I lost her, too." I shake my head. "Don't think like that, Luna Patrice is tough and she has you. Everything will turn out in your favor I know it. You're a good guy, Miller."

My last statement makes him chuckle. "Thanks, I think."

Two days later, I stop by the studio to do a wellness check on Kam. Apparently, John came by to ask Kam to paint his engagement photo of him and Bridget, yes, THAT Bridget. He had the audacity to ask and luckily, I caught the aftermath because I've been chomping at the bit to let Dalila clamp on his windpipe and Calliope to peel him like a banana.

I round the corner of the block where her shop is when I hear the recognizable voice of Kayden Miller.

Wow, he finally came into town. He usually sends someone to pick things up for him so this must be something serious, *but he's in Kam's shop what could he possibly need there?*

When I peek in, he's at the counter purchasing one of her paintings and a tube of paint. Kam is smiling a mile wide and being coy.

Oh my Goddess…she was flirting!

With my Alpha...oh...my...heavens! I rub my eyes to make sure I wasn't dreaming this and that's when Kam puts her number in his phone, while giggling, and she keeps touching his arm.

"What in the name of all that is holy?! Is this happening?!" I can't help but squeal. I do a little dance catching the attention of a guy passing by, he just smiles. And what a gorgeous smile he had but this was more important.

Kam hands him his receipt and I go to open the door, my eyes meeting his knowingly, as he smirks and walks out.

N: Alpha...I'd bow but it would be a lot to explain to my best friend. Nice to see you in town.

He walks past replying on the pack link,

K: Had an emergency to take care of and I'm so glad I did. Talk later, Vanderbilt.

Feigning shock, I play it cool as if I don't know him.

"Holy shit, Kam who was that walking sex god?!"...

Turns out Kayd had asked Kam out on a date. The next morning Kam raves to me about how perfect he is, *here we go*, she is smitten. But instead of being worried, I'm oddly content with this pairing, who knows maybe it could work. Kayden may give off the classic Alpha presence but deep down he is a big teddy bear with an equally big heart, just like Kam.

Who Is He?

I spend the next few days working doubles to cover the rush. I balance several plates on my person and approach a table of guys. Not a bad looking bunch.

"Alright, I have three double cheeseburger platters all medium rare with fries. A Philly cheesesteak with fries and a chicken wrap with a side Caesar salad." A laugh slips my lips as I put all the plates down. The entire table became instantly silent.

Uh oh…what did I do?

"What's funny about my order?" I look right into the deep almond-shaped hazel eyes of quite the specimen. The depth of his voice is beautifully deep. I have to calm the fire burning within me and act professionally.

"It's just different than all the carnivores at the table, is all. You guys enjoy your meal and let me know if you need anything else." I give a smile and turn to check on the other tables but not before a quick glance at the mystery man.

I feel my breath quicken and my palms start to sweat as I break eye contact but not before he throws a panty-dropping smile and a wink.

Though he's sitting down I can tell he is at least six feet tall, he has his locs pulled back revealing shaved sides, it's a rebellious statement to the current trends. His hair is deep black, it almost looks like it has an underlying blue tone. His skin is the color of café-au-lait with tattoos up and down his arms. Still, the most revealing feature is that smile of his, it seems to melt my heart among other things.

I quickly remembered him from when I was dancing outside of Kam's shop and now, he is here.

I walk to the back to catch my breath and make sense of it all, what is happening?

After a while, I notice they have left me quite the tip. I start counting it when I see a slip of paper,

We meet again, beautiful, give me a call 555-9101 Christian.

I open my phone to a blank text message, why the hell not?

N: Hi, this is Nessa, the waitress from earlier.

C: I was hoping to hear from you, beautiful. How about I take you out some time?

N: Listen, I got to be honest, I haven't had the best luck in men lately, so I need to ask, are you married? Kids? Notorious serial killer? I'm honestly tired of the lies.

C: O... kay but no to all your questions and you see, you just hadn't met me yet. I consider myself quite the prize.

N: Oh yeah then why aren't you snatched up yet? Mr. Quite the prize...

C: Because you haven't answered me yet, so what do you say, dinner?

I pause and look at the conversation, he's smooth but there's something about him that is appealing, well besides him being incredibly sexy.

Fate can't be so cruel as to give me a third strike so close together, can it? I mean it's fair to want to rip someone to shreds for breaking your best friend's heart, that shouldn't count against me.

N: Sure, why not...when?

C: I'll let you know...Take care, gorgeous.

I fantasize about that smile of his, feeling butterflies, knowing I am going to go out with this devilishly handsome guy. Somehow it feels different than any other date I've had so far. There seems to be something special about him.

Eventually, Kam went on her first date with Kayd and they seemed to hit it off quickly. It wasn't rocket science to figure out that Kam is indeed his mate. What wonderful news! A big step up from that pathetic disappointment called John Michael.

They have been steadily dating for a few weeks now and that isn't even the best part.

The best news was now I don't have to hide who I was from my best friend.

I wait patiently for her to return from staying over at the packhouse last night, needing to get the juicy details but when I hear her door slam. I rush over there promptly from my apartment. First, the door slam was not a good sign and secondly, I have a feeling she needs me in some way.

I close my door and open hers to see her pacing the floor pulling at her hair, her most obvious sign of frustration. I sit down while Kam stays lost in her own world, she is not in a good way.

I break the tension, "So, I'm sure you have some questions for me?"

Kam turns around so quickly; she seems shocked that I am in her apartment. I can see the hurt on her face, but I didn't know I had a part in it.

"Why didn't you just tell me *what* you are? It wouldn't have changed the way I felt about you, you're my best friend, I love you."

I pull the pins from my updo to let my hair fall past my shoulders and down my back, as my hair turns snow white it blows in the wind but we are inside, there is no breeze. It's thanks to Calliope, my internal diva fan. I smile at Kam's amazement.

We spend the rest of the time finding out about each other because Kam was astonished to find out that she herself is no mere human but a Legacy, the Moon Goddess's most precious being.

She has the mark of the pack and feeding below that is the mark of the Violet Legacies. Indeed, my best friend is beyond special, she has been hand-picked to do great things for our pack. I am so much more excited that now we can do pack stuff together.

A week, maybe two weeks later, Kayd whisks Kam out of town to a cabin by the woods for a very romantic and special weekend. I am super excited to go shopping at Victoria's Secret with Kam to buy some much needed sexy items for her getaway. I'm looking for lace, sheer, corseted, tight, and fitted. I want to leave that man breathless at the very sight of her. Oh yeah, she deserves to be ravished!

When I hand her the fifth outfit, she looks at me, "Nes, it's only a weekend!"

I look at her while trying to find her size in a red silk nightie, "Every girl needs options, besides, what you don't use at the cabin, you'll use at home!" Kam doesn't argue with my logic because I'm right.

Friday night after working another long shift I am so happy to see my bed, we would be practically inseparable this weekend.

Just as I get comfortable my phone lights up and buzzes.

C: Are you up, gorgeous?

N: Just laid down, long day at work. How are you? Hope your business travel went well.

C: It did. I'm just missing that beautiful face of yours, I'm sorry you had to work so hard. How about I take you to dinner tomorrow and sweep you off your feet?

N: Mmm...absolutely, I'll see you tomorrow. I'll send you my address.

C: See you tomorrow, sweet dreams.

I send him my address...my actual address, apartment and all. Even I'm shocked, not even hesitating to hit send though.

This Time It's Different

The next night I find myself staring at the contents of my closet, "What to wear...what to wear?" I am in full-on panic mode as I FaceTime my best friend.

I'm glad I hear rustling as she brings the phone to her face.

"You're so lucky I'm not busy right now." Kam rubs her sleepy eyes.

"Kam, I--I don't know what to wear! This feels different, nothing I have is good enough for this date and it's too late to go shopping! I'm going to have a panic attack!"

Kam sits up, "Hey, calm down, anything you wear he is going to love but if you don't feel like anything is up to par just go to my closet. Now, I know what you're going to say, I dress like a school art teacher, but this teacher has a few risqué options of her own, trust me. Now go into my closet."

I go into Kam's place and into her closet. "All the way in the back, the left side behind my graduation gown." When I slide the graduation gown out of the way I am met with several tight little black dresses and a few wrap dresses that are anything but tame, some are mesh, some are sheer, and some are scandalously short.

"Wow, where...when...how..." I look at Kam who is smiling.

"I learned from you; I just don't talk about it. Anyway, look at them and pick whichever one you want and have a great time. I want details about it later."

As Kam is waving around, I notice something flash on her hand when she widens the shot.

"What was that?! I saw that! Is that a... Kamari... OH MY GODDESS...are you guys engaged?!!!"

She stills her hand to confirm and I scream at the top of my lungs, waking up Kayden.

Oops.

He turns around to see the shock on my face.

"She saw the ring?" She nods and he sits up and kisses her shoulder.

"Hey Nes."

I'm too overwhelmed as I just wave my hand and I start to get teary-eyed.

"Vanessa Ann Vanderbilt, are you actually crying?"

I shake my head as I wipe my face. "NO! Just a little dusty in here." I pull myself together and then smile back. "I am happy for you guys, really." Kayd nods and turns back around to go to sleep.

I shift my focus back to the task at hand. I look at all my options before making a conscious decision.

"I'm going to take the black lace bodycon dress."

"Did he actually say where you were going?"

"No. Anyway, I got to run, doll! Love you guys and we'll talk about the details later."

We blow each other a kiss and end the call.

I take the dress and head back to my place. After a glorious hot shower and pampering, I am ready to take his breath away. Just as I'm about to put on my peep-toe pumps there is a knock at the door. I quickly slide into my shoes and stagger to the door. Before I end up face planting, I grab the knob.

I stand up and inhale slowly trying to gain my composure. Once sure, I open the door and my jaw nearly drops. Christian is wearing a black button-down and fitted black jeans, topped off with a leather jacket. His sexiness seeping from every inch of him as he leans against the doorway biting his lip as his eyes catch my outfit choice. He smiles and his dimples deepen as he hungrily eyes me over.

That's right, take it all in.

"Wow...you look breathtaking..." He takes my hand and spins me around slowly appreciating every square inch of my body. "Wow...just wow. You ready to go, doll face?"

I tease as I bend down to grab my sweater in case it's chilly wherever we are going. I bend at the hip and not at the knee and I hear a faint growl.

I always wondered; guess I got my answer.

I stood up quickly, "I guess I don't need to figure out if you're a werewolf or not, huh?

He shifts, "What gave it away?" As his eyes go black, he smirks further emphasizing his sexy dimples.

"I believe the low growl as I bent over was a dead giveaway. The eyes a close second." He blinks and they are back to his normal color.

"Well, if you only knew what we were thinking to go along with that..."

I can feel Dalila stirring. She's whimpering, signaling she wants something. Oh, brother what is it?

D: I think...that's our mate...I'm so drawn to him I just want to be underneath him writhing in ecstasy.

N: Quiet you! This is a date we don't even know him; he could be a serial killer!

D: Mate not killer, only killer good looks. Possible killer di--

N: Okay! Enough of you...

Dalila smiles before she skips away.

Christian clears his throat to grab my attention. "You okay over there?"

I nod pushing that thought out of my head.

Mate? We don't do the mate thing. Kam, the lovable sweetheart, that's her thing. I am just out here to enjoy life and have fun! Right?

I start to doubt my own thoughts and words. Even though we have just met I am strongly attracted to him and feel like I'm in a trance. I can't pull away, I don't want to, either.

He holds out his hand and I do a little hop skip before connecting my hand with his. He leads the way out the building into his BMW SUV, black of course.

"Let me guess, your favorite color is black?" He helps me into the vehicle, it's a bit high for me and in this scandalous dress, I didn't want to flash him…yet.

"It completes the brooding mysterious look I'm going for; besides, it looks damn good on me." He closes the door.

D: I bet you look good naked too! Mama's going to find out soon! Find out his wolf's name, please?! I need to know what name to breathlessly scream out later...

I sigh and roll my eyes, sometimes Dalila is wilder than I am. I'm interrupted when he hops in and closes the door, hitting the push-start ignition and it roars and then it's whisper quiet. I have to ask, or she'll badger me until I do, let's get this over with.

"Christian, can I ask you a question that's not too forward?" He puts his arm around my headrest leaning further into me flashing that damn smile.

N: Dear lord help me...

I needed a brief reprieve as I looked down for a second, "My wolf would like to know your wolf's name. Her name is Dalila." I notice one of my favorite artists is playing on his playlist. Color me impressed because he isn't well circulated, yet.

"Sure, his name is Kasilious, but I call him Kas. He's been dying to know, too. I guess Dalila is a no-nonsense girl..."

I try to hold it in but I can't and I burst out laughing, "You know that kind of sounds like an ancient plague that the bubonic plague evolved from...sorry I couldn't help it!"

He looks at me with salacious eyes. "It's Greek, baby, and means full of energy, which definitely fits us in every way possible." He winks and I know he can see my full body blush and goosebumps.

D: OMG even his name is sexy. Mate him! Mate him now! I need to do things to him and I want him to have me screaming his name over and....

N: ALRIGHT, I got it. You like him, when did you get to be so depraved?

D: When it mate, not depraved, just love and pure emotion. Dalila loves her mate, Kas.

N: How are you so sure he's our mate?

D: Feel bond, don't worry eventually stupid human will, too. Then Dalila will be right, as usual.

The audacity! How dare she talk to me like that?! Rude!

Guess What...

"Hey, darling, we're here."

I don't even realize we've arrived, too busy squabbling with Dalila. But I glance around noticing we are parked at an elegant restaurant downtown.

"Christian, it's beautiful. But, why here?"

He presents a fragrant long stem red rose.

Okay, he's laying it on real thick.

"For a breathtakingly beautiful woman. Thank you for agreeing to this date, I wasn't so sure after you asked me all those strange questions but I wanted to show you that there are good guys who want nothing more than to give you the world and make you part of theirs."

He knew just what to say. "Yeah? Let's go, I'm starving." I place the flower back in the car and he takes my hand, walking toward the restaurant.

He graciously opens the door for me, and we walk up to the host. He tilts his head but Christian nonchalantly shakes his head signaling him not to say something. The host clears his throat.

I wonder what that was all about?

"Ahem, good evening and welcome to the Green, please follow me to your table."

We walk back into the restaurant to a quiet area. The host begins to pull out my chair but the look on Christian's face is a clear tell to back off.

Christian fixes his face and I act like I don't even notice.

"Oh, I thought the host was helping me with my seat?"

He pushes my chair in slightly and kisses my cheek. "He had to go back to his duties besides I'm the one supposed to be making an impression on you, not him."

During dinner we find out that we share a lot of likenesses, including the love of horror movies and the quest for the perfect nacho. I find out he is an only child like me and that he also has a love of vintage sports cars, he actually owns a classic 1967 Ford Mustang, one of my absolute dream cars.

While waiting for dessert, he takes my hand, his expression serious. Why is my heart starting to beat fast?

"Nessa, I need to tell you something and I don't want it to scare you away." He takes a deep breath and I smile to calm his nerves but internally I am panicking.

Oh no, he does have a big secret. He's probably in a cult or part of a gang that tortures blind people, or a serial killer!

Okay, Nessa, too far. Just listen.

"Nessa, you're... my mate, my beautiful girl who makes my heart pound and my stomach fill with butterflies. Kas has been buzzing in my ear since he saw you and I have been trying to ignore him, but the more I talk to you, the more intrigued I became and I knew you were something special."

He smiles as he squeezes my hand. "I was content with being the lone rebel who didn't need anything or anyone until I met your gorgeous eyes outside that studio, I couldn't wait to see you again. I was so lucky to go to the diner and find you working there. I guess the Moon Goddess kept putting me in your path for a reason and I am glad she chose someone beautiful, smart, and kind as you. I can tell you've been fighting these feelings too and I want you to know we can take it slow, you don't have to say anything just know that I'm already in love with you, Vanessa."

My heart melts at his declaration and when he touches my cheek, I shut my eyes and let go, indeed I feel the sparks and tingles of my mate.

Oh my Goddess I just found my mate!?

I gasp and the tears cascade down my cheeks as I am wrapped in this overwhelming comforting feeling of love. I still can't utter a word as he squeezes my hand, observing my reaction, letting me have my moment.

I never want this moment to end, the moment I've fallen in love.

Separately, we aren't traditional in any sense, but our love is no different than Kam and Kayd's. Well, now everything Kam said makes sense.

After a moment I shake my head smiling, "Look at me, I'm a mess! This is so not me."

He wipes my tears and gives me a heartwarming smile, "You're my beautiful mess, though. My girl..." He leans in to grab my chin and places a sweet kiss to my lips. It feels like fireworks going off in my body and I want more, so much more.

"I've been dying to kiss you since I met you. I can't wait to mark you and make you mine." He was not one to mince words much like me.

I slowly cross my legs as I lean forward, placing my hand on his upper thigh and he jumps as I trail upward.

"Then let's go..."

I'm a breath away from his lips before I ghost them, smiling devilishly. I stand up, using my flirtatious walk to taunt him further before I look back then stroll out of the restaurant.

Christian tosses two hundred-dollar bills on the table as his eyes stay fixated on my every step, rushing to catch up.

Before I can reach for the car door, he's opening it for me. He attacks my lips and I can't help but wrap my arms around him. The kissing intensifies as he pushes me against the car, shutting the once open door. His strong arms encircle my body and his hands travel south, gripping my ass, making me yelp to the strength of his hands.

"I hope I'm not being too forward." He smiles, squeezing once more.

"No, it's fine, in fact, I like when my ass is smacked." I stick it out for him, granting him permission and he does not hesitate to put a good hit on it making me yelp, then I bite my lip to suppress a moan as I exhaled.

He pants loudly, "Sweet Moon Goddess, don't do that baby, that's Kas's weakness, he'll have no problem taking you in the back seat of this car. Just give me the strength to make it to my place." I agree as he opens the door again and I hop in.

We arrive at a three-story townhome on the outskirts of town. It's in a quiet cul-de-sac and fairly new, with dark green highlights to the brick facing. It's obviously one of the new pack properties.

He opens my door and before I step out, I lean back to grab my rose thereby raising the dress up a few inches that I really didn't have. I hear his growl of appreciation as I regain my posture.

"Easy, lover boy. You haven't even seen what's underneath...yet. Now show me your place."

Tease

When we walk in, I place my heels by the door and tiptoe around. Curiosity leads me straight back, passing the living room on the right and the study on the left. I find myself in the kitchen, an open concept with center island and beautiful gray marble detailing. He also has a breakfast nook and a massive deck that overlooks a decent sized yard, *and can probably add a pool,* I thought.

"I did think about adding a pool." He shrugs as I smile at the similar thought we shared. I walk past him, back out the kitchen and up the stairs. At the end of the stairs there were several doors to the right and double Italian doors to the left, obviously the master bedroom.

He sneaks behind me wrapping his arms around my waist, nuzzling my neck causing me to squeal.

"There are three guest bedrooms and a bathroom that way and of course my room over here." Still wrapped around me and no sign of letting go, he nudges me towards his room. I place each hand on a handle and push the doors forward.

Inside, the room is painted a dark grey with black accents. His poster bed is centered in the room and encased in black silk sheets and a gray down comforter, he hasn't made his bed so I get a firsthand account of what he slides into at night, what a sexy bypassing thought.

"Guess I should have tidied up a bit, but I promise, your mate is no slob."

I notice a bookshelf; curious I walk closer only to realize that it's filled with some of my favorites. In fact, I have read a large portion in his collection. I sit in the chair next to the shelf flipping through my favorite book then clutch it to my chest.

"Christian, this is my favorite book ever!"

"See, you were meant for me." He takes my hand as I set the book down. He leads the way to his master bath that includes a rainforest shower and a jacuzzi bath.

"We'll be taking advantage of that shower real soon, love."

I shudder when his lips touch my neck making their way down and over my shoulder. A moan slips and he knows he has me.

I turn to face him after pulling the zipper of my dress down. I let the delicate lace slip off my bountiful curves to pool on the floor.

"Mmm, Christian...I need you."

His mouth drops when he gazes upon the rose gold lace set. The bra barely covered my ample breasts, they almost spilled over the top deliciously. I seal the deal with a moan and a bite of my lip.

Done.

Kas takes over and slams me against the nearest wall. His eyes black as coal as he paws me.

"Mate! Need mate..." He growls.

The passion brings Dalila to the surface and now two carnal beasts are acting out their sexual tension.

The wild creatures, in human flesh, growl as they use their claws to rid each other of their clothes. When Kas rips my lingerie set, Dalila pauses and looks at him sideways, he knows he will be buying a new set.

Kas picks Dalila up and she wraps her legs around his waist as she pulls his hair to get more access to his neck. That gesture makes him growl sending shivers up her spine, he likes that, noted. She tugs harder before he tosses her on the bed which is super soft. She bounces before she lays there in wait.

I gain control back as I blink rapidly. "Mmm, please..."

My eyes meet his intense hazel gaze. He stalks me, climbing on the bed slowly. My eyes fall to what I am looking for.

Whoa.

N: Holy...hell, he might rip me in half, I've never seen one so...big.

D: Mate perfect fit, get ready for many orgasms.

Dalila is salivating at the site of her mate's naked form but I'm still a tad concerned.

Christian looks down and sees my worry but smiles.

"Don't worry, love, it'll be a perfect fit...but first I want my lips on yours..."

He kisses my inner thigh getting closer and closer to his goal.

OH. MY. GODDESS!

I arch my back, lost in pleasure as he finally hits his mark, making me convulse almost instantly. There is something about his touch that my body reacts to so suddenly and craves more.

I've never reacted that quick before, but he is my mate, perfect for me in every way especially sexually. And in this moment, he takes advantage of my surprise and flips me over onto my stomach, straddling me behind my ass. He leans forward placing kisses all over my back, each one a spark that ignites my fire.

"Christian, please..." I'm desperate for his touch, I'm wanton.

"Tell me what you want, Vanessa." His deep sexy voice whispers in my ear.

Even my name on his lips is incredibly sexy. I am drunk on him and he knows exactly what I want but he wants me to beg, beg for the relief I so crave.

"Mark me, Christian. Make me yours and only yours. I've never wanted someone as much as I want you... I need you."

I glance at him over my shoulder. I know he sees my gaze filled with lust. He pulls my hair to the other side holding it tightly making me gasp. He whispers in my ear, "Gladly, I'm yours and you're mine."

You're a What?!

With that he sinks his teeth in quick...and deep.

"Son of a bitch! What the hell, you didn't have to go so deep, did you? I thought that's reserved only for..." I stop abruptly.

I turn around to a smug smiling Christian. "You were saying?"

I shake my head,

No way, none of the signs were there, were they? Was I blind to it all?

To be honest, most of our interaction was over the phone.

Would Kayd have known he was here? Had he met him already?

There are so many unanswered questions pouring in during this very intimate moment. I can't let it go; I need to know.

"H-have you met Alpha Miller?"

He nods laying on his side.

"Always, anytime I visit another pack's land I always pay my respect to the Alpha..."

"But you own a house here?"

He chuckles adjusting the sheets.

"I was granted permission to by Alpha Miller once I explained to him that I sensed my mate was part of his pack. This is hopefully just a vacation property. I have to get back to my own."

I'm shocked, there's no possible way he could be...

"Who are you?"

He smiles that smile that melts my soul. He takes my hand and kisses it so gently.

"Christian Grey, Alpha of the elusive and mysterious Midnight Shadow Pack. But more importantly, is who YOU are going to be. You, my dear, are soon to be Vanessa Grey, Luna to said pack."

Whoa.

I'm floored, to say the least, I didn't sense it and he wasn't giving off any signs.

An Alpha, my mate is an Alpha! I'm just speechless.

"Sweetheart, say something."

"How, how did I not catch on? I thought I knew all the nearby Alphas?"

"Well that's probably the problem, I live on the northern border in California. Not too far from here but technically not nearby. I hope that's not a problem?"

California?! I love California! I have always dreamed of living there, laying on the beach in my tiniest of bikinis and just listening to the ocean. This is perfect! But...I still have so many questions.

He places his finger on my lip. "Shhh...I can see that pretty little brain of yours trying to absorb all this information but later for that...My sole purpose now is to hear my name from your lips."

He hovers over me but I'm still in shock, I would never have guessed my mate would hold power over an entire pack and now I have the responsibility of caring for them all. I am definitely going to need a chit chat with Kam ASAP! Kam hasn't been Luna for long but still, it's longer than me, obviously.

I'm brought out of my thoughts once again when his lips trail a fire along my body.

"Fu--Christian..."

"Just like that, baby. Say my name just...like...that..."

A Last Wild Night

Later, cuddled up in the sheets, he kisses my forehead and pulls me closer.

"I know this is still a shock, but I have never been so sure of anything in my entire life. I can't wait for you to meet the pack and see the packhouse, you can even redecorate it and make it your own."

I trace my fingers across his chest, "How close are we to the ocean?"

"It's a boardwalk away and we're kind of on a cliff too so the sunsets are magical. I can't wait for you to see your first one with me, nestled in my arms, as the sun gives way to the moon to brighten the sky."

I sigh, "Me, too."

He looks down at me and he looks like he's surprised by what I said.

"Really? I thought I would have to do some major convincing or maybe even have to kidnap you."

I shake my head, squeezing him tighter, "No, it doesn't have to come to that you see as much as I adore my small hometown and all it has to offer, I love visiting new places, I sort of have the travel bug. Besides, my best friend has her mate and she'll be busy with the pack business and creating a family, she'll be so happy that I have settled down, she has lots of wild stories of Vanessa, the party girl. Anyway, seeing her and Kayden together has made me want something like that, it was time for something more and here you are." I watch his expression, he seems perplexed, but then he smiles.

"So, Luna Kamari is your best friend? Well, how fitting, she can help you adjust but I already know you're going to be an amazing Luna. I still want to take things slow; we can talk about moving and quitting your job, you don't have to work another day in your life. Anyway, you should start your Luna training as soon as possible and as long as the pack is at peace, I will whisk you away to anywhere in the world."

I sigh heavily, "I know it's a lot to take in, but I think I can do it. I can't wait to spend my life with you and our pack but only on one special condition..."

He raises an eyebrow but then nods. I place my hands on his chest and smile, "You have to let the party girl have one last wild night in her hometown with her friends at her favorite bar."

He sits up, contemplating her offer. He leans over and grabs something from the bedroom dresser beside him. He opens it, "Only if you promise to wear this so they know that this party girl is spoken for."

I gasp looking at a stunning rose gold diamond in a gold band. I don't know how many carats but it's huge!

"Christian, it's...it's beautiful! I--I don't know what to say!"

"Just say yes to being my girl, my wife, the wild party girl turned future mother, doesn't matter how you label yourself as long as you say yes to spending your life with me."

I raise my eyebrow at him, "You just happen to have an engagement ring with you?"

"I told you I knew my mate was in this pack, I had to be prepared."

There goes that damn smile. I inhale deeply then throw him my own smile.

"Then yes, I would love to be the future Mrs. Christian Grey and Luna of the great Midnight Shadow pack!"

The Future Mrs. Grey

*T*hree weeks later, Christian comes back to claim his beauty. He failed to tell her when he was coming in and she figured he would call or text, but he had other plans.

I felt warm, all cuddled up in my blankets dreaming of my bad boy Prince Charming when there is a knock on the door. Refusing to get up fast enough the knock becomes irritatingly louder and harsher, like the police. I throw off my blanket and stomp down the stairs.

"I swear, this better be the...what?!" I swing open the door to face a huge bouquet of flowers.

"Delivery." Said the man behind the vase.

"Oh my gosh, these are so beautiful...but no card. Hmm, I bet they're from Michael, wait no Corey he loves spoiling me with things like that..."

The man's still holding the flowers and listening to me ramble until a low growl slips from his direction.

"Babe, come on, I know it's you, your scent gives you away, remember? Thank you for the beautiful flowers, just put them on the counter. I need to brush my teeth before greeting you properly."

He sets them on the counter and sits on the couch while I go into the master bathroom. He lets his head fall back against the couch and he sighs. He definitely had an early morning flight since it's early morning here. He drifts off into sleep until I place my lips to his. He opens his eyes to see me smile.

"Hi, baby, welcome home." I moved into the townhome while he was back conducting pack business and getting the house ready for my arrival. All my essential items from my apartment were shipped there already. I only brought clothes and toiletries to the townhouse.

Kam moved out of her apartment almost immediately after finding Kayd, so it was no big deal when I moved out of mine.

"Thank you, baby, but anywhere you are is home, I missed you."

He pulls me over the couch so I'm lying in his lap. I pull a blanket over us and burrow closer, his scent is intoxicating. "I definitely missed you. She helps but she just doesn't do it like you do." I hold up my left hand and he can't help but laugh.

"Well, she's missing quite a few things including length and width. We'll have to do something about your needs...soon." His kiss ignites my soul and I feel a switch turn on inside me.

"Christian..."

He stops to look at me, "What, no Michael or Corey?" He attacks his mark on me and I'm panting.

"No...no, only you baby, only you. Chris...stop teasing me, please." He licks and nibbles his mark further coaxing a moan from me.

"Say it..."

I'm a mess and willing to do anything he asks. "I'm yours, baby, all yours." He grins wickedly before carrying me upstairs.

Get Ready

"Yes Kam, be there at 9pm. Ooooh, really? I can't wait to see the dress; I know you'll do me proud. Okay, tell Kayd I said hi and Chris sends his love, too. Bye!"

It's midafternoon and Christian is out getting dinner, breakfast, and snacks for tomorrow, predicting the inevitable hangover. Tonight, is my farewell party because in two days I will be starting my new life in California as Luna of the Midnight Shadow Pack with my fiancé, the very sexy bad boy, Christian Grey.

I'm going through all the normal emotions I'd expect since I've made the choice to accept Christian's proposal, but I know that where he is, is where I am supposed to be.

I start my prep early, 6pm, blasting my music as I hop in the shower. I take time to wash, shave, and exfoliate every inch of my body.

I dry off and put on my silk robe while I tweeze my brows and apply a face mask. With my feet moving to the music, Chris walks in, eyeing me. His expression amused.

"Take a good look, are you willing to see this every day?" I joke as I rub the seaweed and aloe mask over my skin. He takes my hand and places the leftover on the bridge of his nose and cheeks, I laugh so loud.

"If it makes me as breathtaking as my wife, I want to try it, too. I'd love seeing this every day, no, I'd just love seeing you every day. Now that I found you, when I went back to the packhouse it seemed wrong with you not there, it felt empty and incomplete and you've never even set foot in the house."

"And this place felt so cold without you, I drug Kam over the first night because I was so terrified and felt so alone without you. Let's just say Kayd was not happy with me but I told him I had her first. He had no argument after that..."

I start to wipe it off, but he takes the warm towel from me and gently wipes away the mask revealing a canvas of glowing skin.

He smiles, "Ahh, there's my beautiful girl."

He wipes his face clean and touches the skin where it was. "Wow, that feels amazing, I may have to do that more often with you but in private, can you imagine if one of our pack members saw me downstairs in the kitchen with it on?"

I laugh at the thought, "Oh my gosh, they would think I had turned you into a big softie, but we know that isn't true. You're strong, fearless, and ruthless when need be and quite the animal in bed, but they don't need to know *THAT* part. Mmm..." I snap out of my daydream and he's showcasing those dimples.

"We can have a little fun before your party, you know." He pulls me in, his lips tracing my smooth skin.

Why must he tempt me so?

"As much as I would love that, darling, it's after 7 and I'm still in my robe, I still have to do my hair and makeup and you have to make us a snack while I get ready..."

I flash my charming smile, "Please, baby, I'm all yours tonight, especially if you make me some pizza bagels." I start to untie the knot in my belt and his focus immediately follows the movement. The fabric parts revealing a super sexy lace balconette bra and boy shorts in his favorite color, black.

His hands wrap around my bare waist as he growls and bares his teeth, Kas is trying to take over. He shakes his head and gains control. "Sorry, doll face I almost lost it. You shouldn't tempt me with that, we'd never leave the house."

I pout and bite my lip, "Can I have pizza bagels please?" He kisses my forehead, "You can have anything you want; I'll be back, you finish getting ready." He smacks my ass catching me by surprise. Now tingling all over, I want him bad, right now.

I start on my makeup, carefully crafting the bombshell look I found on Pinterest with a bold green smokey eye and a light pink lip. I add lashes and finish it with a finishing mist to seal it all in.

Christian walks in just as I finish, "Hello, lover." I use my seductive voice and he almost drops the plate.

"Damn, baby! Is this what you usually do before you go out, I don't know if I want guys to see you like this."

"Easy there...this look is especially for you, I found it on Pinterest. I thought it would look amazing. You just confirmed how right I was."

"Pin, what? Whatever the case you look so sexy, baby. How much longer?" He sets the plate on the counter and I pop one in my mouth and I'm surprised when he kisses me immediately. "Judging by my hair? Probably 45 minutes."

"Jeez, all I need is like 30 minutes for everything."

I glare at him. "That statement was completely unnecessary, go get dressed. Remember, I am the guest of honor, so I have to look smoking hot to catch everyone's attention and that's what I plan to do."

He sneaks back up on me and bites my shoulder, "That's fine, it'll be my name on your lips later tonight, anyway..."

He walked out without another word and I was panting at the very thought of it. My entire body temperature rose twenty degrees and he barely touched me. I must focus if I want my hair done soon so I pump up the music and work faster to curl my hair.

Christian takes the guest bathroom to get ready, he decides to switch it up a little and wears a blood-red button-down with his black jeans and boots. He unbuttons the top two buttons to show a hint of his broad muscular chest and he rolls his sleeves up to expose his powerful arms and tattoos. He couldn't wait for after the party he had a surprise for her. He spritzes on her favorite cologne and does a once over before heading back to their room.

He can hear her singing along with the songs and it makes his heart skip a beat, the song is a love ballad and she once told him it reminded her of him. She doesn't know it but it's to be the first dance at their reception. Like Kam, she had a Luna ceremony, but she also requested a wedding for tradition's sake. He stands by the door for a moment just to listen.

She had a songbird voice and he could listen to her all night.

When he steps forward, I smile but continue singing and getting ready.

"I'm almost done, promise." I reply in between lyrics. He wraps his hands around me and rocks me from side to side while gazing at me in the mirror. "I know, I just want to hold you. I haven't seen you in three weeks." I do my best to maneuver my hair with him wrapped around me. Once I'm content with the look I was going for, I tousle my hair in place.

"Wow, you look like my own personal Jessica Rabbit, I can't wait to see the dress." I lean back, close my eyes and smile. "I missed you so much and I don't want this moment to end." For a moment we bask in each other and then I open my eyes to see his still closed. "Wake up handsome, I need to get dressed." He sighs defeatedly before finally opening them, the hazel color seemed to pop against all the dark colors he wore. "Okay, I'll meet you downstairs." I lean back for one more kiss before he leaves to let me get ready.

Wow...

Downstairs, Christian is texting his Beta, Fitz about the status of the pack.

Fitz: Pack is fine Chris, same as it was a few hours ago when you asked. You should be enjoying your time with your fiancée.

Chris: I am. I was just curious to what was going on there.

Fitz: She must be getting ready for her party and you're bored, so you bother me about "pack business", admit it!

Chris: What are best friends for man? I swear she was half-naked and was already smoking hot. I don't know how I'll make it through the night with all eyes on her.

Fitz: You'll be fine; besides, it seems like she is the type to tell people and show off, so she'll have no problem flashing that ring around especially if any ex's show up. It'll be a big fat 'so there' to them. Just have fun and enjoy letting her say goodbye to her small-town life and embracing the one she'll have with you.

Chris: You're right, man. Okay, we'll see you in a couple of days then.

Just as he wraps up his conversation, he can hear my feet coming down the stairs. His jaw drops so far, I'm not sure if it will ever go back to its original position. I walk down the staircase. I am wearing a white lace mini dress that would definitely cause a scene on anyone but on me it is lethal. I paired it with black sandal heels that have a bow on the back and a black clutch purse. I look at him for approval.

"So, does this look okay?" I ask, feeling a bit hesitant, hoping he likes it.

"Oh baby, you just don't know how fucking sexy you look! Now I really don't want you to go anywhere but I promised you, so let's go." He kisses my cheek conscious of my lipstick. "Come on, Mrs. Grey, your celebration awaits." I grin from ear to ear, oh how I love to hear him call me that.

We pull up to the bar and he steps out to open my door. I graciously accept and pull my dress down, noting that when I was seated it rose several inches. We lock hands and walk towards the entrance.

"Hey Zeusy!"

He sighs and rolls his eyes. "You know you're the only girl I allow to call me that, how's my baby girl

I haven't seen you in a while?" He looks over at Christian, who holds me a bit tighter. Zeus smiles from ear to ear. "Has my little one finally settled down?"

I gleam showing him my engagement ring, "I have and tonight's the last night of partying for me and then I'm off to Cali with my love, Christian. I'll miss you so much, Zeus." I tear up when I call him by his actual name.

He pulls me in for a father style hug. "It's Zeusy to you, little one. You take care out there and don't be a stranger. And you, take care of my girl, she's like a daughter to me and I'll have no problem burying you in a shallow ditch."

Even Christian seems a bit intimidated by Zeus, he's a big man, the perfect type for security. "Yes, sir. My angel will always be protected by me, I give you my word." He nods and we head inside.

We head towards the VIP section where I see Kam and Kayd, standing but in each other's arms. They are making out and so I clear my throat loudly. Kam turns around to reveal a semi-sheer black dress that hugs her every curve and a pair of killer black heels. Damn, I've taught her well.

"Well, no damn wonder he had you all pinned up! You look stunning, darling!"

We hug and Kam takes a good look at me, "Who knew I'd see you wearing a white dress, albeit a short slutty one but soon it'll be the wedding dress of your dreams." Kam tears up and I can feel my own tears forming.

Kayd sighs loudly, "Good grief here they go...let's go grab a beer, man." The guys walk to the bar to get drinks as we try to compose ourselves.

"Nes, I'm so happy for you, who knew we would fall in love around the same time?! I'm glad to continue sharing these experiences with you and I am so glad to call you my best friend and my sister." We hug again and the tears fall, and we realize we were going to ruin our makeup and quickly regain our composure.

"So now what?" I give her that devilish smile, shooting up my hands, "Shots!"

Mine

We saunter over to the bar to run smack dab into Colby and Briar, both are working tonight. I knew there was a great chance to see one or the other but not both. It was disarming to feel my stomach sink with Colby after our...situation.

Kam looks over at me, sensing my uneasiness, "Hey, we can go to the other bar, it's okay."

I relinquish, "No, because we're going to be here for a while, and it'll have to happen eventually. I'm definitely going to order four shots."

We saddle up to the bar and Briar comes over, "Hey, doll face! Nice to see you guys it's been a while, what's been going on?" He's preparing our shots without us even saying anything.

"Well, funny you should ask...this is my farewell party. I'm going to be leaving Lovenshire in two days with my fiancée. He's Alpha to the Midnight Shadow pack in Cali."

Briar's mouth drops, "Shut! Up! I'm so happy for you, Nes! Let me see that ring, girl!" He gasps loudly as I reveal the beautiful piece picked by my beloved.

All the commotion sparks Colby to come over. "What's with the squeal...oh, hey Nessa, how are you?" There was a slight tension in the air. I pull my hand back over the bar.

"Good, Colby, I hope you are too."

He nods. "So, what's the squealing all about?" Kam and Briar both look at me to spill the beans.

"Uhhh...so this is my farewell as well as my engagement party. I'm headed to California with Alpha Christian, leader of the Midnight Shadow Pack. I wanted my last party to be where I had the most fun."

He smirks, you could see a tinge of hurt hearing the news. "Congrats, Nessa, that's wonderful news. Sorry, I should get back to work." He walks away to tend to the next customer.

Kam pats my back, "Don't worry about him."

Briar squeezes my hand, "Listen, he took the breakup bad because he knew he did wrong to a great girl, girls actually...even when we were messing around I suppose he always wanted to get a second chance, especially after his fiancée left him but you don't worry about that, this is a celebration and I better get an invite to the wedding...now, here are your shots, one for Kam and four for the wife to be. Cheers and bottoms up!"

We clink our glasses and slam down the shots.

"WOOOOO! Spring Break! Yeah!"

Kam just shakes her head. "Same old crazy times Nessa!"

Four shots later I headed back to our area with a smile on my face, I was feeling good. I spot my sexy man-beast talking to Kayd and his friends Brent, Evan, and Miles. That man exuded an undeniable sexiness!

The guys congratulate him on our engagement and have the usual guy talk. I, slightly tipsy, saunter over and sit on Christian's lap with a plop.

"Oof! Hey, baby."

He gazes at me and I immediately kiss him, my hands all over him. I could feel him shifting and he pulls me in closer. After a few moments, he pulled back and I was eyeing him hungrily, "I need you...now." I wiggle in his lap, feeling around. "and you obviously want me, too. Can we go?" I whine and continue wiggling. He groans and holds me, so I sit still.

"Doll face, I promise you after this I am all yours in every possible way your dirty little mind can imagine but this is your time to hang out with your friends before you start your life with me. Go, have fun, drink and dance and then later..." He whispers in my ear causing me to moan, cursing under my breath. My eyes were overflowing in lust, I'm rocking against him, this time in need, not to be a tease. He mouths the word "later" and I nod. He taps my ass, so I stand up.

At the same moment Kam and I's song comes on and the DJ dedicates it to me, congratulating me on the engagement. Kam stands up looking for me and we step away from where the guys are seated but still close enough to give them a show.

I pull Kam into me and we grind on each other as we sing the lyrics, if anyone didn't know any better, they'd think we were together as we caress each other. I seductively grind into Kam and vice versa. Every move was calculated as I only stared into his eyes. It was a sexy dance for my man without being lewd.

Christian peers over at Kayd who has his eyes locked on Kam as she shook her hips side to side against me, giving him a sneaky wink when her eyes finally meet his, she has been avoiding his gaze on purpose. His grip on the chair was apparent, she has set herself up for the same night that I am planning to have. After the song is over, we do another round of shots before the next good song comes on.

Though I've had eight shots and counting I am still surprisingly functioning. I, once again, plop down on his lap. He keeps his drinking light as we are planning to take an Uber home, and someone needs to give the driver the address. He's on his third beer when I hop on.

"Hey." I smile giving him a peck and it causes him to smile.

"Hi, lovely, having fun?"

I nod, "Thank you for letting me have one last night of fun in my hometown, it means a lot to me."

"You're welcome, anything for the love of my life."

I stop and stare, overwhelmed by his words. My eyes fill with unshed tears, "Oh baby, I love you so much. I can't wait to be your wife."

Alright, safe to say I had crossed the threshold to lovey-dovey drunk.

We whisper to each other, to us there was no music, just each other. After a few more rounds and a few more hours of dancing, everyone was ready to call it a night.

Kam hugs me for the longest and then pouts, "When will I see you again?!"

"I'll be at your wedding, remember? Don't fret bestie, Christian has a private jet and I'm only an hour and a half flight away and vice versa if you want to visit me. I love you so much!" We drunkenly hug and sway to no music.

Kayd takes her hand and she waves goodbye as they head to their Uber that was waiting for them.

Christian orders our ride and he turns to me, I was staring at him, but not exactly *at* him.

"Were you looking at my ass?"

I smile coyly with a finger in my mouth. "No... maybe..."

He pulls me into him, and I squeeze his ass, it's so hot. "Nice."

He drops his hands to my lower waist, his fingertips gently caressing me. "It's okay, I spent the entire night doing that, you danced so sexy I wanted to sneak away immediately, I almost followed you to the bathroom but you girls do that group thing."

I laughed "Oh, such a naughty boy, you could have too. I would have enjoyed you in a bathroom stall with no regrets." His jaw drops at my confession and he growls before nuzzling into my neck.

"Wonder what they would think of the Alpha and his Luna canoodling in a club bathroom like that?"

I shrug my shoulders, "What we do in our off time is none of their business and if I want my Alpha to take me at a club then that's what is going to happen. Our love is just as rebellious as we are, so don't expect us to be ordinary in any way." I grin as I pull him in for a heated kiss.

We get distracted until the driver calls him. "Come on, let's get you home for part two."

When we get home, he lets me open the door while he attacks my mark. I try to concentrate on such a simple task but can't due to the overwhelming passion coursing between us.

Forever Etched

Finally, I get the key in and turn the knob. I start to walk away but he slams the door and then pushes me up against it for a full uninterrupted make out session. His hands are canvassing my body not only for pleasure but to find the damn zipper! He wants me naked as soon as humanly possible. I sense his urgency and take over, slowly starting to unzip myself as I walk toward the stairs. He is close behind as I have the zipper all the way down, but I hold the dress together as I walk toward the bedroom. He pushes me up against the wall next to the entrance and I reach over to open the door.

I walk toward the bed before I allow the dress to fall revealing the set from earlier, it is still sexy as hell. He curses under his breath. I wait for him to pounce on me but he's slow to react.

"I thought you'd be on me by now?"

He unbuttons his shirt and lets it drop. "Oh baby, I would be, but I have a surprise for you." He piqued my interest and he motions with his finger for me to come to him. He leans down for a deep, passionate kiss before pulling back. He turns around to reveal a bandage on his upper right shoulder. The bandage was about the size of a magazine, the contents under it unknown.

"Chris, what is this?"

He looks back and smiles, "Well I decided to get this when I was back home, it's just something I wanted to have so that if you're not around that anyone will know that you're mine and I'm yours. It's okay, you can take it off."

He shrinks down so I can remove the bandage, I'm careful due to its sheer size. I peel slowly to reveal a fresh tattoo. The dark black ink is a contrast to his warm skin tone. I remove the final inches and gasps.

"Christian, baby, it's...probably the most beautiful thing ever."

He has vines surrounding the date that we met and below that he has inscribed, *'I'll love you forever, my Vanessa, my party girl. You are mine and I am yours, CG'*

I'm in tears, it's overwhelming. No one has ever dedicated something so personal, so painful, and so permanent to me. He is my one and he wants the whole world to see his profession on his body.

He turns around to face me, "So, what do you think?"

Without a single word, I push him against the door, and he lifts me, so my legs wrap around him then he takes me to our bed. His kisses trail from my lips to my belly button. I'm already a moaning mess after teasing each other all night.

All our clothes are thrown to the floor and we are tangled up in the sheets for hours, appreciating every inch of each other. Soon we will be christening our bedroom at the packhouse but for now, our oasis in my hometown is all we need. He is mine and I am his...

Into the Future

18 years later

"Looks like Kam recommended a great housekeeping service to keep the house up while we were away, they did a great job. It looks like it did the first time I walked through the door."

I head back into the kitchen as Christian lugs the luggage into our bedroom upstairs.

I love this kitchen layout, so much I had the one back home remodeled to this very concept, though the color of the tile, backsplash, and floors are different it still gives me that open feel that is better in a house full of people.

I open the fridge to eye our options since I had them deliver food to the house this morning. We will be having an early dinner tonight; I know my hubby will be starving after waking up early to fly back so we can be rested before my god children's 18th birthday and change of power ceremony.

Kayd is retiring and passing on the pack to his twins to share the power. It has never been heard of before and this is the event of the year because of the circumstances.

I heat up the cast-iron skillet for the steaks and warm up the oven to bake the dinner rolls. I am as comfortable here as I am at home. It took me a few days to get used to the massive amount of people wandering around the packhouse but eventually, I realized it is like I inherited an enormous family.

He made good on his promise and took me out to watch my first sunset overlooking the cliffside and ocean below, it was magical just as he said it would be. The breeze gently swayed my white summer dress as he wrapped his arms around me and dipped me just as the final rays settled into the horizon, it was a perfect moment.

In fact, that's where we held our wedding. A small but meaningful affair as my sister, Kam was my matron of honor.

It took some time due to a threat on the pack but a year after our wedding on our anniversary, I surprised Christian by wrapping up my pregnancy test as a gift. I will never forget the shock on his face when he opened the box. He looks at the test, then me, then the test again and this time he looks at me with tears in his eyes.

"Really?"

I nod and place his hand on my growing belly. "Yes, really."

Seven months later I gave birth to our son, Xander Christian Grey. Now at the tender age of 16, he is on his way to taking over his pack as well and is in intensive Alpha training for the summer and can't attend the ceremony of his cousins. I tried to convince Christian that a few days break wouldn't hurt but he insisted that Xander's training is crucial to the survivability of the pack. I'll make sure to let his cousins know how proud he is of them.

The meat instantly sizzles, bringing me back into the present, searing in the hot pan as I ladle butter and rosemary over it constantly until they are medium rare. Now I sauté the asparagus in the leftover butter and plate it just as the dinner rolls were golden brown. I put the plates on the table and went looking for him.

I find my love, resting, his head tilted back leaning against the couch. He is still quite the rebel, age never played a factor on his fashion sense or hairstyle, he still keeps his sides shaved. Plus, he still has a passion for wearing mostly black. I just love my bad boy.

I take the opportunity to lean down and place a gentle kiss on him. When he opens his eyes, mine meets his. "Hey, dinner's ready, let's eat and then take a nap afterward before the party."

He smiles, "Just a nap?" He wiggles his brows and I laugh that he is still the same after all this time.

I pull him up, "If we have time, come on let's eat."

THE END.

Excerpt from A Christian Tale:
Bound Series #3

"It's bad enough I think she's on *their* pack land, she's...affiliated with my enemies but...this could work to my advantage. My precious little mate doesn't have to know everything. She just has to be on my side when I lay out my plan of attack on the "great" Cheshire pack. Her love will bind her to me no matter how devoted she is to the pack and if she fights it, I'll reject her and it will *kill* her, literally. She'll be too in love to go against me though, this **WILL** go as planned no matter how long it takes."

-Christian Grey

Stay in Touch!

Email: **authormskeiya@yahoo.com**
FB Author Page:
www.facebook.com/authormskeiya
Instagram:
www.intstagram.com/author_mskeiya
Bookbub:
www.bookbub.com/profile/s-courtney

Website (sign up for updates!):
scourtneybooks.yolasite.com

Please look out for the rest of the Bound Series and much more from S. Courtney

THE BOUND SERIES:
    Bound to You (#1)
    Bound by Destiny (#2)
    Unapologetically Nessa (#3)
    Blood Bound (#5)

CHARACTER BACKSTORIES:
    A Christian Tale (#4)

    # indicates release order

OTHER WORKS (Titles subject to change):
    The Black Aces MC
    Do You Want a 'Cup of Coffee?'
    Remember Me?
    It's Our Anniversary